Tab

Chapter One 1
Chapter Two 7
Chapter Three 11
Chapter Four 19
Chapter Five 25
Chapter Six 29
Chapter Seven 33
Chapter Eight 37
Chapter Nine 41
Chapter Ten 45
Chapter Eleven 51
Chapter Twelve 57
Chapter Thirteen 63
Chapter Fourteen 69
Chapter Fifteen 75
Chapter Sixteen 81
Chapter Seventeen 85
Chapter Eighteen 89
Chapter Nineteen 93
Chapter Twenty 97
Chapter Twenty-One 103
Chapter Twenty-Two 107
Chapter Twenty-Three 111
Chapter Twenty-Four 115
Chapter Twenty-Five 119
Chapter Twenty-Six 123
Chapter Twenty-Seven 129
Chapter Twenty-Eight 135
Chapter Twenty-Nine 139
Chapter Thirty 145
Chapter Thirty-One 149

Chapter Thirty-Two 153
Chapter Thirty-Three 159
Chapter Thirty-Four 163
Chapter Thirty-Five 167
Chapter Thirty-Six 171
About the Author 173
Other Books by Billie Houston 175

Asking For a Miracle

By

Billie Houston

COPYRIGHT BILLIE HOUSTON 2014
All Rights Reserved

This is a work of fiction any similarity to real persons, places, or events is purely coincidental. All rights reserved.

All scripture quotations are from the King James Bible.

Chapter One

August 1974, Friday Afternoon
Carole Garner pulled her car into the drive, and stopped the motor. "You don't have to do this."
Midge Adams shifted in her seat to look at her friend. "I know that, but I'm not about to abandon you after all these years. Are you up to this?"
Carole wasn't. She didn't know if she would ever be. Her recently deceased Great Aunt Effie was so much more than an aunt. She was the only mother Carole ever knew, and the only family she ever had. Carole was six months old when her parents died in an automobile accident. What would her lot in life have been if Aunt Effie hadn't stepped in and given her a home? "It has to be done, and I am the one who must do it."
"No, you aren't," Midge argued. "There are a number of organizations that would clean Aunt Effie's house and haul off what's inside for free."
Carole looked at the craftsman bungalow. It was on a corner lot and nestled among several stately oak trees. A lump rose in her throat, as nostalgia tightened her chest. This was not just a house. It was a home. She grew up here. How many times had she walked up and down those porch steps, on her way to or from school? She and Aunt Effie had shared so many Christmases, Easters, and Thanksgivings here. Memories swept over her like a rising tide. She put her hands over her face and sobbed before regaining her composure enough to speak. "Aunt Effie would look down in horror if she thought strangers were pilfering through and hauling away her belongings."
Midge leaned closer, and put an arm around her friend's shoulders. "Don't cry, Carole. Aunt Effie was ninety-four years old. Her health was failing. She's in a better place now."

After another struggle with her emotions, Carole gained control. "It's hard for me to realize she was that old." A disturbing thought crossed her mind. "Aunt Effie was forty-three when I came to live with her. She was seven years younger than I am now. If my daughter was seven instead of seventeen, and I was faced with bringing her up alone, I'd panic." Once again, her tears flowed. "She devoted so much of her life to me. I never told her how much I appreciated all she did for me, and now it's too late."

"I often heard her say that you coming into her life gave an old spinster something to live for. She loved you. I can speak as an authority since I grew up in the house next door to you." Midge reached for her handbag and pulled out a tissue. "Wipe your eyes, and let's get started. We have a lot of work to do."

*****

August 9, 1974
Friday Evening

The ring of the doorbell disturbed Jack Garner. He laid his book facedown on the table beside him and went to answer. He swung the front door open. "Otis? What brings you out at this hour of the night?"

Otis Thorpe scratched the side of his head. "I live across the street, not across the country. I come bearing good tidings. Did you hear the news?"

"I heard. I'm surprised you consider Nixon resigning good news." Jack stepped back. "Come in." He followed his old friend through the foyer and into the living room.

"I don't. That's not the good news I'm talking about." Otis dropped into Jack's favorite chair.

Jack settled on one end of the couch. "It's good news to me. The guy's a crook." They had debated this subject so many times before.

"He's a politician. What else do you expect?" Otis's homely features screwed into a frown. "All politicians are crooks. That's how they get to be politicians. That's not why I came over. I got an invitation today to the Texas Korean War Veteran Association's Twenty-First Anniversary Convention over at the Lone Star Hotel in Mason City. It's on the first weekend in September. I'm going. Would you like to come along?"

Jack had spent the last twenty-one years of his life trying to forget Korea and everything that happened there. "I'd have to talk to the wife first."

"Where is Carole?" Otis looked around the room. "And your daughter?"

"Suzie is staying overnight with Cindy. Those two are inseparable. Carole is out somewhere with Midge, I suppose. I called Midge's house and nobody answered."

"You called Midge? That has to be a first." Otis leaned back in Jack's recliner and smiled.

"Cut the comedy." Even though Midge was his wife's best friend, and had been since they were children, Jack didn't like the woman.

"This is Friday," Otis reminded him. "Maybe the two of them are out taking in a movie, or shopping or maybe they decided to go streaking." He guffawed, "Now, that would be worth seeing, Midge Adams streaking." On a more sober note, he asked, "What kind of president do you think Gerald Ford will make?"

"What we're getting couldn't be worse than what we had." Otis' remark about Jack's wife registered. "Carole would never dream of streaking."

Otis held up his hand. "I was teasing. Don't go getting huffy with me." He stood. "Talk to Carole and let me know if you want to go to the convention. We have to register by August twenty-third."

Carole burst through the front door, carrying a ledger under each arm. She pushed at the door with one foot. "Jack, give me a hand please."

Jack hurried to assist his wife. He took one of the ledgers. "What are these?"

"Hi, Otis." Carole came into the living room, laid the other ledger on the couch, sat down beside them, and kicked off her shoes. "I don't know. I found them at Aunt Effie's. They were locked in a safe hidden behind that portrait of her father that hangs over the fireplace in the den. We didn't find the safe until late in the afternoon." She rubbed her fingers across her forehead before running them through her hair. "It was so late by then, I decided to come home and peruse them here. I didn't want you to worry."

Carole's recently deceased aunt had been eccentric, to say the least. Jack laid his ledger atop the other and sat on the far end of the couch. "How did you manage to open the safe"?

"The combination was in some of the stuff Aunt Effie left for me to read. We had a terrible time making it work, but Midge finally got it open."

Otis grinned. "Too bad Effie didn't stuff the safe with money. Did you hear the latest, Carole? Nixon resigned as president."

"I heard. Midge brought a radio with her." Carole put her hand over her mouth, and yawned. "I'm beat. I'm going to bed."

"Before you look at these?" Jack tapped a ledger with one finger.

Otis stood and moved toward the door. "I gotta go. I have to get up early tomorrow." He paused, his hand on the doorknob. "It costs fifty dollars a person to register for the Korean Veterans' Convention. That includes breakfast, lunch, and dinner for Friday and Saturday. Maybe Carole and Suzie would like to go too. When you decide, let me know. I'll make the arrangements." He opened the door, and paused again. "I'm planning to go on Friday, stay the night Saturday, and then drive back Sunday morning. If you want to ride with me, I'll make your room arrangements too."

Before Jack could answer, Otis was out the door and gone.

Jack stood and extended his hand toward his wife. He couldn't imagine Suzie wanting to go to a veteran's convention. On second thought, maybe she would. He could never second-guess his daughter. It would be good for Carole to get away for a weekend. *It's been such a long time. Surely by now—stop it!* "Would you and Suzie like to spend the Labor

ASKING FOR A MIRACLE

Day weekend in a nice hotel?" He waited for a reply, half-hoping she would refuse.

She caught his hand and he pulled her to her feet.

"I would miss Sunday morning services, but it would be nice for us to have a family weekend together. I could meet some of your war buddies."

"Both you and the Baker Street Baptist Church will survive one Sunday without your presence. I'll tell Otis to make our arrangements. Did you complete your work at Aunt Effie's house?" They walked up the stairs, and toward their bedroom.

"I hardly got started. I had no idea she had so much in the house, or that sorting through it would be so painful. It made me realize for the first time, Aunt Effie's gone, really gone, and she's not coming back."

"Would it help," Jack asked, "if I went over tomorrow and sorted through some of the things in the garage?" He opened the door to their bedroom, and waited for Carole to enter before following her inside.

"And miss your golf game?"

Did he detect a touch of resentment in her voice? "Is that your way of saying you don't want my help?" Before the words were out of his mouth, he regretted saying them. Carole was still recovering from the trauma of her aunt's death. This was no time to renew their longstanding argument over his Saturday golf games. "I didn't mean it like that." He sat in an upholstered chair in the corner. "I'm sorry."

Carole sat at her dressing table and then pulled a brush through her long hair. "It doesn't matter."

It did matter to Jack. She had been his wife for twenty-five years. They were married almost a year when he was drafted. He spent the next two years in the hell that was Korea, living in bunkers, dodging bullets, killing to keep from being killed and... *It's over, and has been for long time. Forget it.*

The first few years he was home were rocky ones. His mother, sister, and Aunt Effie were contributing factors to their difficult readjustment.

BILLIE HOUSTON

Midge belonged on that list too, and Otis. Time passed. A miscarriage, another pregnancy, and the death of their new-born son gave then some emotional maturity. Then Suzie came along. Their daughter was bright and beautiful, and healthy. Things got better. Maybe it took them that long to grow up and learn to compromise, and to tell in-laws and good friends to butt out of their business. He was comfortable now in his marriage. He liked the status quo, and intended to maintain it. He took off his shoes and pushed his socks down into them. "I'm going to take a shower." He detoured on the way to the bathroom to give Carole a peck on the cheek. "I'm sorry."

She smiled into the mirror. "I'm sorry, too. I appreciate your offer to help, but this is something I have to do myself. Can you understand?"

"Sure I can." He didn't understand. Why argue over something as trivial as Aunt Effie's belongings? "Give yourself a break. Don't go near that house until Monday." He closed the bathroom door behind him.

Chapter Two

August 10, 1974, Saturday Morning
Carole woke early. She opened her eyes as events from yesterday played through her thoughts. She dressed quietly, being careful not to wake Jack as she slipped into a pair of worn jeans and a cotton tee-shirt and then brushed her hair back into a ponytail. Streaks of gray had begun to show through the chestnut brown at her temples. *Maybe I should consider a rinse. Maybe I should get a haircut.*
Her mind moved to the task ahead. Aunt Effie saved everything from Christmas cards to old newspaper clippings. How was she to decide what to keep and what to toss?
She tiptoed from the room and went to the kitchen where she made a cup of instant coffee and wrote a note for her family.

> *Dear Jack and Suzie, If you need me, I will be at Aunt Effie's house.*

She should apologize to her husband for making a snide remark about his Saturday golf game. How many times had she promised herself she would stop her nagging? Too many, but she continued to complain. Saturdays should be family days. Jack wasn't a family man, not after he came back from Korea. After those war years, there was a part of him she could never reach. She once thought he might change with time. She knew now he never would.
The telephone clanged. Carole answered before the second ring, hoping it hadn't awakened Jack. "Hello."
Carole pulled the phone away from her ear and winced as Midge's voice blasted into her ear.

"Something has come up. Don't go near your Aunt Effie's house until I can go with you."

"Don't shout. Is it something bad?"

"No. Something good. Something very good. I'll explain later. See you Monday. Love you, bye." Midge hung up the phone.

Carole shook her head. Midge never ceased to surprise her. *I have other, more pressing things to do this day.* She walked through the living room, picked up her purse and the ledger numbered as one. She wouldn't have Midge for company. Maybe the ledger would provide some entertainment during rest breaks.

Thirty minutes later, Carole pulled into Aunt Effie's drive. She had stopped at a fast food place and bought a burger and fries. She could make coffee here and not have to go somewhere for lunch.

When she went inside, the emptiness grabbed her like an unwelcome hug. The heat was oppressive. She put her bag and the ledger on the couch and hurried to adjust the thermostat. Cool air blew out through the vents. She looked around the room and thought of the task ahead of her. *You can do this. Aunt Effie wants you to do it. She expects you to do it.*

Carole sat on the floor before the bookcase in the den. One by one she pulled the books from the bottom shelf. *David Copperfield, The Secret Garden, Tom Sawyer, Hans Brinker or The Silver Skates, The Blue Book of Fairy Tales, A Child's Garden of Verses, Little Women.* She stopped and stared into space. These were the books Aunt Effie read to her when she was a child. Sentimental old fool that she was, she couldn't part with them.

She brushed the dust off each one and put it back in its rightful place, before moving up to the next shelf. It held Aunt Effie's books. *The History of Ancient Greece, The Rise and Fall of the Roman Empire, Strong's Bible Concordance.* Several books by Victoria Holt, *Sonnets from the Portuguese,* Aunt Effie's Bible. She had to stop. Tears blinded her vision. *I can't do it.* Giving these books away would be like giving away precious memories. She dried her eyes on the tail of her T-shirt and put the books back on the shelf.

What I need is a strong cup of coffee. She went to the kitchen, filled the coffee pot, and then sat at the table while she waited for it to perk.

She loved this kitchen. The room was cozy with updated counter tops and appliances. The table, like always, sat along the east wall under a row of windows. Carole smiled as she recalled the memory of Aunt Effie buying the table from a second hand furniture store. It took her weeks to sand and refinish it. She showed off her handiwork to all the came through the front door. *I can't do it. I can't strip Aunt Effie's house and sell it. Neither can I rent it.* She couldn't bear the thought of someone else living here.

She swiped away her tears and took a cup from the cupboard. Even the coffee cup aroused memories. It was the one Aunt Effie always used. Carole poured her coffee, and moved to sit at the table. She stared out at the back yard. *I have to do what I have to do. Jack is going to think I've lost my mind.* He would no doubt say she couldn't keep the house. *It's my house. I can keep it if I choose to, and I do.* A heavy weight lodged in her stomach. She drank her coffee, went to the living room, and sat on the couch. Her work in this house was done. Suzie had often talked about finding an apartment when she started college next year. Maybe she and her friend Cindy would like to live here. That would please Aunt Effie. *Have I lost my mind completely, trying to please a dead woman?* A small voice in the back of her head argued, *she's not dead, she has moved on to a better place.*

Aunt Effie was the strongest woman I ever knew. Her voice, inaudible, yet clear as a bell rang in Carole's mind. *Christ is my strength. He sustains me day by day.*

I have to get out of here. I'm not only talking to myself, I'm hearing answers. She thought about going home. Suzie would be off somewhere with Cindy. Jack was on the golf course. There was no point in going

BILLIE HOUSTON

home to an empty house. She picked up the ledger, and turned to the first page. The words that stared back at her made her gasp.

The Journal of Mary Elizabeth Effington.
AKA Effie Doud.
Born August 10, 1880, in Cedar Gap, Texas
Daughter of Thomas Henry Effington
And
Mary Agnes Doud Effington

Chapter Three

August 10, 1974. Saturday Evening

Jack laid his unopened newspaper in his lap. Where was Carole? He had skipped drinks and dinner with the boys to come home early. What did he find? An empty house.

It was time he did a little fence mending. He had stopped at the florist and bought a lovely bouquet of spring flowers. He would take his wife to dinner tonight.

He called Midge to see if she knew where Carole was. Midge didn't answer her phone. He opened his paper, but he couldn't concentrate on reading it. His mind kept straying.

The telephone rang. He tossed the paper aside and took his time getting to the clanging instrument. "Hello."

"Who are you angry with now?" His sister Margie's voice sounded in his ear.

"I'm not angry"

"You sound angry."

Jack sat in the straight chair near the telephone table, and sighed. "What's the problem?" Margie never called unless there was a problem.

"It's not a problem I hope. Mother says we should have a family barbeque on Labor Day. She's invited Abigail and Martha since they are widows and neither of them has any family to speak of, no one that speaks to them anyway. She will pay for the meat. You can do the barbequing. Carole can—"

"Hold it," Jack bellowed. He added in a much calmer voice, "Carole, Suzie, and I will be out of town on Labor Day."

"Where are you going?"

That was none of Margie's business. Despite that, he told her. "Texas Korean War Veterans are having their annual convention over in Mason City."
"Why didn't you tell Mother?"
In his mind's eye, Jack saw his younger sister with her red hair curling around her face and her green eyes filling with tears. "It never occurred to me she would make plans for a gathering at my home without consulting me first."
"Mother has invited guests. She's even given them directions to your house."
"She can have the barbecue at her home." How could his own mother give a barbeque at his home, then assign him a ton of work to do without discussing her plans with him first?
"She's going to be upset," Margie said, "she will have the granddaddy of all hissy fits."
"All she can do is rant. Ignore her," Jack replied.
"I hate it when she's angry with me."
Jack rubbed his forehead and drew a deep breath. "Margie, you are forty-seven–years old. Stop behaving like a child. Take charge of your own life."
"First you yell at me, and then you hurt my feelings."
Jack apologized. "I'm sorry." Margie was a pain in the neck sometimes, but she was his only sibling and he loved her. He understood her as no one else could. She was a middle-aged woman with the emotional maturity of a teenager. She'd been married and divorced twice, and her third husband, although a nice enough guy, had left her more than once. "Where is Steve?"
"We're separated again." She sobbed into the phone. "This time he may not come back."
"Don't cry sweetheart. I'll call Mother and straighten out this Labor Day misunderstanding."

Margie sniffled. "Thank you, big brother. Bye." She sniffled again and then hung up the phone.

Jack knew there was no point in postponing the inevitable. He picked up the phone and called his mother.

It rang several times before she answered. "Garner residence. Clarissa Garner speaking."

"Mother, this is Jack."

"Oh?"

Clarissa Garner used words the way some people used blunt instruments. Jack cringed as he felt the impact of her first blow.

There was reason to beat the devil about the bush. "Carole, Suzie, and I will be out of town over the Labor-Day weekend."

Suzie and Cindy came rushing through the front door, making enough noise to wake the dead.

"Hi, Dad."

"Hi, Mr. Garner."

Jack covered the receiver with his hand. "Please, girls, I'm on the phone."

Suzie paused long enough to kiss his cheek. "Where's Mom?"

Clarissa's voice was loud in his ear.

"Jack, for heaven's sake, what is going on there?"

"I don't know where your mother is," Jack called to his daughter's retreating figure. "I'm trying to talk to your grandmother."

"Oops, sorry," Suzie called over her shoulder as she and Cindy disappeared up the stairs

Jack turned his attention back to his telephone conversation. "Sorry for the interruption."

"You should keep a tighter rein on that child, Jack. She's out of control." Arguing with Clarissa was like winking in the dark. "I'll take your advice under consideration."

"You are so much like your father, God rest his soul. Did Margie call you?" After a short silence, Clarissa demanded, "Did she?"

He was not up to this. "You know she did." When had Margie not done exactly what Clarissa told her to do?

Her voice cut like a knife. "Despite that, you went ahead and made plans to go out of town?"

Any explanation would be an exercise in futility. Nevertheless, Jack did explain. "I made my plans before Margie called."

"This is no way to treat your mother." She slammed the receiver down, breaking the connection.

There was a time when Jack would have called back. Not anymore. Learning to walk the fine line between standing his ground and disrespecting the woman who gave him life was a never-ending battle.

He was scarcely settled with his book when the telephone rang again. He answered immediately. Maybe it was Carole. "Hello."

He heard the clipped voice of a telephone operator as she spoke in measured tones. "Long distance from Las Vegas calling Carole Garner." Carole didn't know anybody in Las Vegas. "Carole isn't here. This is Jack Garner, her husband."

The operator addressed the person on the other end of the line. "Carole Garner is not able to take your call."

"Oh, pooh."

That was Midge Adams' voice. What is she doing in Las Vegas?

The operator asked, "Would you like to speak to Jack Garner?"

"No way." Midge hung up.

*****

Carole read the last page of the second ledger, and closed the book. The silence of Aunt Effie's house wrapped around her like a shroud. *What I have just read can't be true.* Nevertheless, she knew it was. Twilight darkened to night. Darkness crept into every corner of the room. *Where do I go from here?* Common sense told her that question would have to answer itself. *From the beginning, my life has been a lie.*

ASKING FOR A MIRACLE

Jack opened the front door and tramped into the room. "You promised me last night that you wouldn't come here today." His face was a thundercloud of disapproval.

Carole remembered no such promise. Last night happened to another Carole in another place that was far away and eons in the past. "I read the ledger I brought with me." Her voice echoed in her ears sounding as vacant as her heart felt.

Jack sat on the couch beside her. "What's in this thing?" He took the ledger from her lap and thumbed through it. "Who wrote in it?"

In the silence of a gathering twilight her reply resonated into the darkening room. "My mother."

"Your mother has been dead fifty years. This leger doesn't look that old." Jack switched on the lamp beside the couch, opened the book, and perused a few pages before lifting his head. "Aunt Effie was your mother? That would make her forty-three years old when you were born."

"Forty-three years old and unmarried. I'm a bastard."

Jack laid the ledger aside and put his arms around his wife. "You are no such thing."

She pulled free of his embrace. "Yes I am."

"Why would Aunt Effie spin such a yarn?"

"In nineteen twenty-four being unwed and pregnant marked both a mother and child for life. She may as well have been wearing a scarlet letter on her chest. I would have suffered a worse fate. I'd have been an outcast, at least that's what she wrote."

Jack rubbed his chin with his thumb and forefinger. "Who was your father?"

Oh, how Carole wished she knew. "That's the one thing Aunt Effie didn't tell. She told the circumstances, but not the name."

"What were those circumstances?" Jack leaned forward with an expectant look on his face.

This had been Aunt Effie's secret for over fifty years. It was Carole's secret now. She intended to keep it. "You must never tell this to a living soul, not ever. Do you promise?"

"You can't keep this a secret. Like murder, sooner or later, it will come out."

"Aunt Effie didn't want anyone to know.

"Carole, really"

"Who are you angry with now?"

"Promise me."

Jack shook his head. "Your Aunt Effie is dead. She won't know or care what you tell."

"My Aunt Effie is in heaven. She's looking down, watching everything I do."

"Honestly Carole, for an otherwise sensible woman, you carry this religion business too far." He stood, shoved his hands into his pockets and stared down at her.

"Don't call Christianity a religion. It's not." Why must he start in on her, now of all times, about her Christian beliefs? She swallowed her anger. "I am a witness for Christ." Anger would not help her cause, and Jack was right. If she hoped to find her relatives, this was not something she could keep secret, even if she tried. "Sit down, you're making me nervous."

Jack sat back on the couch, stretched his long legs in front of him, and crossed one ankle over the other.

Carole drew a long breath. "Aunt Effie was my father's secretary. They fell in love. The problem was, he was a married man with three teen-aged children. When they learned I was on the way he was forced to make a decision. Did he divorce his wife and marry Aunt Effie, or did he choose to stay with his wife? It's obvious what his decision was."

"He deserted her?" A frown furrowed Jack's brow.

"He supported her financially by providing her with a monthly income until I was born. After that, he set up a trust fund for me. That was our source of income until the stock market crashed in nineteen twenty-nine. My father went bankrupt. After that Aunt Effie sharpened her secretarial skills and went back to work. She was fortunate enough to find a job at the county library. That's where she worked until nineteen fifty-five when she retired."

Jack patted Carole's arm. "This is nothing to be upset about. Put it out of your mind." He stood. "I came to take you out to dinner."

"Nothing to be upset about?" Carole was appalled. "You think not knowing who I am, or if I have relatives I never knew about, is nothing? Suppose my half siblings are still alive? Do I have half-brothers or half-sisters, or both?" She jumped to her feet. "I have to find them or their descendants."

Jack reminded her, "That doesn't fit very well into your scheme to keep this a secret." He took her arm. "Let's go."

Jack was right, as usual. "I know." Her head ached. She couldn't think about this anymore tonight. *I'll figure it out tomorrow.* "I'm ready to go."

Chapter Four

August 12, 1974, Monday Morning
Carole's garden was her pride and joy. She fastened a hose to a faucet, turned on the sprinkler and sat on the patio watching the water whirl around in dizzying circles. Her mind wandered back to Saturday and Aunt Effie's ledgers. She was not my aunt. She was my mother. Why didn't she tell me?
"There you are." Midge came through the side gate and toward the patio. "I rang the doorbell and knocked a half-dozen times." She stepped into the shade. "Where have you been?"
"More to the point where have you been?" Carole pointed toward a metal chair. "I called your house off and on all day yesterday."
"I hate August." Midge sat and fanned her hand in front of her face. "Jack didn't tell you I called Saturday?"
"You called me Saturday?"
"I did, from Vegas." Midge's face lit with a radiant smile. "The most wonderful thing happened over the weekend. Elbert and I flew to Vegas and married. You can now call me Mrs. Elbert Marshall."
I can now call you stupid. "You said it was all over between you and Elbert."
"I thought it was when he walked out on me. He called late Friday night and said he couldn't forget all we meant to each other. He asked if he could come over. At first I said no. He kept insisting until I said yes. We talked until early morning. The rest, as the old saying goes, is history." She clasped her hands together, and rested her chin on them. "I have found my soul mate."
"If I calculate correctly, this is soul mate number four." Midge was such a fool where men were concerned.

"The first three don't count."

"Three marriages don't count?" Her friend was headed for heartbreak again.

"Please, Carole, be happy for me." Midge's big brown eyes filled with tears.

Carole wanted to kick herself. Midge was tiny with a face and figure that denied her age by at least ten years. Men were attracted to her like steel to a magnet. "I am happy for you" Carole reached across the short distance that separated them, and took Midge's hand. "I am very happy." Belatedly she recalled Midge's remark about calling her Saturday. "What did you mean when you asked if Jack told me?"

"I called you Saturday. I wanted to tell you about Elbert and me."

"It must have slipped his mind." Considering all that happened that day, she could understand how it would.

*****

Sunshine chased shadows as the days slid by. The nearer Labor Day weekend drew, the more excited Carole became. She looked forward to spending a night in a plush hotel room alone with Jack. They could forget all the problems and cares that plagued them at home, and share a romantic night. Maybe they could find a spark of passion and rekindle a flicker of romance.

Suzie tore into the kitchen. She never entered a room, she invaded it. "Mom, Cindy is having dinner with us. She's staying the night with me. Is that okay?"

What would she do if just once, my answer was no? "It's okay."

Otis rapped on the sliding patio door. "Can I come in?"

Sometimes Carole became impatient with Otis, but she could never be angry with him. When he and Jack were in Korea he literally saved Jack's life by half-carrying, half-dragging him five miles from the front line to a MASH hospital. Jack had shrapnel in his left leg. He healed quickly, and served a few more months at the front before he rotated and was sent home. "Sure."

Otis came through the back door and into the kitchen. "I made all the arrangements for our Labor Day jaunt. By the way, the Sunday night dinner is formal."

Carole peeked inside her oven. She cooked her roast to perfection, and then used oven mitts to remove the pan and set it on top of the stove. It smelled wonderful.

Otis lifted his head and drew in a deep breath. "That smells mighty good."

"Would you like to stay for dinner?"

"I wouldn't want to impose."

"No imposition." Carole set two more places. "Cindy is staying for dinner. You're guest number two."

Otis grinned. "Those young people are a hand full. They make me glad I'm not a teenager." He snapped his fingers. "By the way, I could only reserve two rooms. The hotel is booked solid. You and Suzie can bunk together. Jack will have to put up with me."

So much for a romantic night alone with her husband.

*****

August 27, 1974
Tuesday Afternoon

Carole sat in a chair just outside the dressing room of Miss Millie's Dress Shoppe's dressing room. When Jack learned the convention's dinner was formal, he suggested she and Suzie buy new dresses for the occasion.

"Ta da." Suzie stepped from the dressing room a strapless gown with a long slit up one side. "How do you like it?"

"On you, I don't. Go back and take it off. Try on the off-the shoulder gown with the bouffant skirt."

Suzie stood with both hands on her hips. "I am eighteen-years-old. It's time I started choosing my own clothes, and not have to wear the little-girl ones you choose for me."

Carole armed herself for a battle of wills. "You won't be eighteen until April of next year. You are not going to get that dress. Forget it and choose something more appropriate."

Suzie pouted. "Aunt Margie wore a gown very much like this one to the Easter Ball. Everyone thought she was beautiful, even Daddy. I heard him tell her so. She agrees with me. I am mature enough to dress like an adult."

"But not like a floozy." Carole drew a deep breath and exhaled slowly. Jack's sister was a bad influence on Suzie. Why didn't Margie have children of her own? She could mess up their heads, and leave my daughter alone. "You can't have the dress. That's final."

Suzie tossed her head, as she sashayed back into the dressing room. Carole knew she hadn't heard the last of this.

Suzie tried on several other dresses. The first few Carole gave thumbs down in short order. After much haggling, they compromised on a gown made from a red floral brocade fabric. It had a V front and back neckline. The skirt was fitted and flared at the hem. It was not what Carole would have chosen, but it was a vast improvement over Suzie's first choice.

Carole chose a pink satin gown with puffed sleeves and an empire waistline. She stepped from the dressing room and stood waiting for Suzie's reaction. When no comment was forthcoming, she asked, "How do you like it?"

"It's not you." Suzie wrinkled her nose. "Let me find something for you."

"No. I like this one."

"Mother, for heaven's sake, it looks like something Elizabeth Bennett, from Pride and Prejudice would have worn. Why is it you get to say what I can wear and I can't even make a suggestion about what you wear?"

Against her better judgment, Carole relented. "Okay, give it your best shot. Find three dresses that are me."

If those three dresses were any indication of how her daughter saw her, Carole was an over-the-hill hippie. She tried on two of them, and hated them both. The third was too terrible to consider. She bought the pink gown.

Suzie sat sullen and silent as they drove home. Carole knew when to keep her mouth shut. They were nearing home before Suzie decided to speak. "It's not fair."

Carole was too experienced in verbal battles with Suzie to ask what wasn't fair. "Nothing in life is."

"Aunt Margie says..."

"Enough Suzanne."

Suzie closed her mouth and stared out the car window

They drove the remainder of the way home in uncomfortable silence.

Chapter Five

September 1, 1974, Sunday Morning
Carole rolled over in bed. Remembrance came slowly. She opened her eyes. The bed across from her was empty. "Suzie?"
Suzie sat in an armchair. "Sleepy head. It's almost ten o'clock. If you don't get down stairs by eleven you will miss breakfast."
Carole crawled from the bed and headed for the bathroom. "Go on without me. I'll be down soon."
"I had breakfast over an hour ago. Since I have no interest in hearing the Korean War being fought all over again, I planned an excursion for us today. We are going to see the sights of Mason City. I picked up a brochure and a city map at the front desk."
Carole showered and put on her underthings. She was pulling her dress over her head when Suzie opened the door. "Not a dress, Mom, wear pants and walking shoes."
Carole turned her back to Suzie. "Zip me."
After all these years, she was about to meet Jack's war buddies. She wanted to look her best. "I prefer a dress, thank you. Where do you plan to go?"
"Our first stop will be Mason City's Cowboy Museum." Suzie pulled the zipper up and stepped back. "It sounds fabulous. They even have memorabilia of movie and television cowboys."
Carole would rather stay at the convention and meet the people Jack knew in Korea. He seldom talked about his experiences there, even after all these years. On the other hand she wasn't crazy about the idea of Suzie wandering around Mason City alone. "I'll talk to Dad."
"You could stay here," Suzie ventured." We could go alone."
A warning bell sounded inside Carole's head. "Who is we?"

BILLIE HOUSTON

"I met this boy who's a son of one of Daddy's buddies. He is interested in cowboys too. He's as bored with this convention as I am."

Carole raised one eyebrow. Suzie was not going to travel around Mason City with some teenage boy she didn't know. "You are not going out with some young man you have just met."

"Oh, Mom, he's not a man. He's a ten-year-old kid. His dad brought him to the convention because he had no place to leave him. His mother died last Christmas Day. Isn't that a terrible day to lose your mother?"

Any day is a terrible day to lose your mother, even if you don't know she is your mother until after she is gone. "Yes, it is. I'm sorry for the boy, but you shouldn't have offered to take him sight-seeing without asking me first."

"I didn't offer. Daddy did."

"When did this happen?" Carole's eyes widened in surprise.

"This morning when we were having breakfast. Nick Armstrong, that's the name of Daddy's buddy, said he would miss some of the meetings today because he was going to take Corey, that Nick' son, to the Cowboy Museum. Daddy said he could go with you and me. He said we'd be happy to have him along."

That was a brazen act, even for Jack. Carole took an exasperated breath. "Your daddy has some nerve, speaking for me."

"Don't be mad at him, please Mom. He was thinking about that poor little boy not having a mother to take him. Corey won't be any trouble. I'll watch out for him. Can he go with us, please?"

"Okay, but don't you ever do something like this again." When they got home, Carole was going to have a long talk with her husband.

*****

September 1, 1974
Sunday Afternoon

ASKING FOR A MIRACLE

Carole sat at a table in a far corner of the Cowboy Museum's cafeteria, and sipped her second cup of coffee. She should have taken Suzie's advice and worn a comfortable pair of shoes. She would have, had she known Suzie and Corey would insist on walking through the huge museum, not once, but twice. After the second tour, Carole called a halt and looked for a place to eat.

After consuming catfish and fries, huge slices of pecan pie, and drinking two glasses of tea each, Suzie and Corey decided they should go for one more look at the museum.

Corey was a shy child. He said nothing to Carole through their two tours. He chattered like a magpie to Suzie. He spoke directly to Carole for the first time since they were introduced. "Could we please, Mrs. Garner?"

"Yes, but don't linger too long. I'll wait for you here." She watched them hurry away. *I'm an old softie.*

The cafeteria was almost deserted. She glanced at her watch. Three-fifteen. Time to spare before this evening's eight-o'clock dinner.

"I beg your pardon. Excuse me."

Carole looked up to see Nick Armstrong standing across the table from her. "Is something wrong? Why are you here?"

"No problem." He put his hand on the back of the chair across from her. "May I sit down?"

"Of course." Carole nodded.

"Where are the children?" Nick scanned the cafeteria.

"They are tramping through that museum for the third time." Carole doubled her fist and pointed over her shoulder with her thumb. "I decided to wait here for them. Were you worried about Corey?"

"Not at all. I am grateful to you and Suzie for including him in your outing." Nick settled in his chair. "I hope he wasn't a bother."

"We enjoyed his company. Your son is a very nice young man. You must be proud of him."

"I am," Nick assured her, "but I worry about him since we lost Mary Ellen, my wife."
"I'm sorry for your loss. Losing someone you love is painful."
"Indeed it is." Nick looked over Carole's shoulder. "Here come our cowboy-loving children."
Carole looked back. "I hope three tours was a charm."
Corey greeted his father with a big smile and a hug. "Hi, Dad."
Nick ruffled his son's hair. "Hi yourself."
"I promised Corey a glass of tea. I could use one too." Suzie took Corey's hand. "Mom, more coffee? How about you, Nick?"
"No thanks." Carole put her hand over her empty cup.
"Nothing for me." Nick shook his head as he pushed his chair back. "We have to go. It was a privilege meeting you. Jack is a lucky man. I thought after he lost Chong Sun and the baby, he might never find anyone else to love. Thanks again for sharing your afternoon with Corey." He stood and motioned for Corey to follow suit.
Carole sat, too stunned to move. A dozen distressing thoughts ran through her head. Chong Sun was a Korean name. Jack lost a baby? No. There was some mistake. He wouldn't keep a secret like that from her for all these years.
"Mom?" Suzie tapped her on the shoulder. "You look like you saw a ghost. Are you sick?"
"My stomach hurts. It's tied in knots." She stood and grabbed her handbag. "It's time we got back to the hotel."
"Are you sure you're all right?"
"Stop fussing over me." *How can my world be all right when it just crashed and burned?*

Chapter Six

September 2,' 1974, Monday afternoon
The moment Otis pulled his SUV into the driveway Carole opened the car door and jumped from the back seat. She was fumbling for her door key, when Jack sat the suitcases he carried on the porch, eased her aside and opened it. He stepped back and waited for her to enter. Something was troubling her. She hardly spoke to him during last night's dinner or through the uncomfortable ride home today. He picked up the suitcases and followed her inside.
Suzie and Otis, each carrying suitcases, followed Jack. Did they feel the tension in the air? Otis must have. He set the suitcases down, said his goodbyes and left.
Suzie headed for the stairs. "I have to call Cindy."
"You can call her down here." Carole sat in Jack's easy chair and kicked off her shoes.
"I like using my telephone." She ran up the stairs taking two steps at a time.
Carole frowned and shook her head. "I still think getting that girl a Princess telephone with a private line was a mistake." Jack's seventeenth birthday gift to Suzie was her own telephone. Carole had objected and she still did.
"We need to give the girl a little space. She's almost an adult." Jack sat on the couch and pushed a pillow behind his back. Something more than Suzie's Princess telephone was gnawing at Carole. "You aren't concerned about Suzie's telephone. What are you really upset about?"
Carole held his gaze in the gridlock of a challenging stare. 'Who is Chong Sun?"

A fist of fear punched into Jack's stomach. He looked away, unable to meet her steady gaze. "Who told you about Chong Sun?" He broke into a cold sweat.
"I wasn't told anything. Nick Armstrong mentioned her in passing."
After all these years... "Where and when did you see Nick?"
"Don't evade the question, answer me."
Her voice was a knife through his heart. Jack half-stood. His legs too weak to support him. He sat back down. *The day of reckoning is here.* "She was someone I knew in Korea. She's been dead for a long time."
"How well did you know her?" Two tears escaped Carole's eyes and rolled down her cheeks. Her tone changed from sharp to quivering.
"It happened a long time ago. I don't remember." He did remember, he remembered all too well.
"Don't lie to me," she cried out.
He bowed his head. The burning in his neck spread to his cheeks. He was damned if he told and damned if he didn't. "There's not much to tell. We met in the middle of a crazy, chaotic war. We had a brief affair. She died."
"What did she die from?" Carole held up one hand. "Never mind, I know. She died in childbirth. Was the baby yours?"
Jack made another attempt to stand. This time he succeeded. "Stop it, Carole, stop it." He put his hands to the sides of his head and paced across the floor, before pausing and turning to face her. "I can't take anymore." After twenty years of guarding it so carefully, his secret was out.
"One more question. This time tell me the truth." She grasped the arms of the chair she sat in. "If Chong Sun and child had lived, would you have taken a leaf from Otis' book, divorced me, and married her?"
"Who told you about Otis and Nari?"
"She did, just before she died." Carole stared down at her hands. "She wanted to confess her wrong doing before she went to meet her maker."

ASKING FOR A MIRACLE

"Otis and his first wife were separated when he was drafted. The circumstances were different." Jack's heart beat like a tom-tom. What happened was irrevocable. Would his wife's knowledge of it destroy his marriage? Please, God, he hoped not

"All these years, you kept Otis's secret, and he kept yours."

"We all have secrets. Sometimes they are best kept." His lie of silence could not be explained away with cunning words. "It's over. It has been for a long time. Please, can we forget it and get on with our lives?"

"Tell me, if she had lived, would you have divorced me and married Chong Sun? Carole hung on with the tenacity of a bull dog. "I want the truth. I deserve that much."

That was the one question he had never asked himself. "It was all so long ago, in another place. One ravaged by war where nothing was sure, not even your next breath. "I—I—It was so long ago. I can't say now what I would have done then, I—"

Carole stood. "You already have." She picked up her shoes, and ran from the room.

Jack followed her as she raced through the den and toward the back yard. "Wait, Carole, let's talk about this." He reached the patio just as she ran through the garden gate and disappeared around the corner of the house.

He caught up to her and grabbed her arm. "Listen to me, Carole. Please listen to me."

She shook free of his hold. "Don't touch me."

"Please, Carole," he pleaded.

"I need some time alone."

"I'll sleep in the spare bedroom tonight." He took her arm again, and this time, very gently, led her back through the gate, and onto the patio. "You will feel better after a good night's rest." He searched for words to say something, anything to ease her pain and his torment. None came.

BILLIE HOUSTON

She freed herself from his grasp, and went into the den. "I am going to Aunt Effie's." She laughed. It was more of a screech that bordered on hysteria. "I'm going to the house my mother left me."

He followed her inside. "You are in no condition to go anywhere." Once again, he reached for her arm.

She struck him hard across his wrist. "Don't try to stop me."

He grabbed his wrist with his other hand. His surprise outran his pain. Carole never struck him before. She never struck anybody. Before he could get his thoughts together, she disappeared up the stairs.

Chapter Seven

September 3, 1974, Tuesday Morning
Carole spent the night in a house filled with too many memories and haunted by the ghost of Effie Doud, or was it Mary Elizabeth Effington whose presence she felt so distinctly?
Around three-thirty in the morning she fell asleep on the couch. Dawn was breaking when she awoke with a stiff neck and an aching back. "I'm too old for this." She stumbled to the kitchen and made a pot of coffee. Her thoughts were if she could be alone, she could sort through her muddled feelings and put her confused concerns in order. No such luck. She was as confused and disturbed this morning as she was when she left her home last evening.
She watched the coffee bubble up and percolate. Today was Suzie's first day of school and she wasn't there. How could she forget something so important? She couldn't send her only child off to begin her senior year alone.
She took the coffee pot off the burner, turned off the stove and rushed back to the living room.
Twenty minutes later she pulled into her driveway. As she came up the steps, Jack opened the front door. "Thank goodness you came home. I was afraid you wouldn't." He stood back and waited for her to come inside.
Carole walked past him without speaking or looking his way.
He followed her into the living room. "And a good morning to you, too."
Suzie came down the stairs bubbling with excitement. "Hi, Mom. Just think, this is the first day of my senior year in high school."

Carole put one foot of the first riser of the stairs. "I'll be ready in a few moments. Grab some breakfast. This will be a long day."

"Mom, we have to talk." Suzie gripped the back of a chair.

Carole took another step upward. "I have to get ready."

"No, you don't. Cindy is coming by to pick me up. I'm going alone."

Jack, who until now stood by in complete silence, said, "Let's go to the kitchen, I've made breakfast. We can talk there." He took his daughter's arm. "I made waffles."

Carole followed her husband and daughter into the kitchen.

Jack extended a hand toward the kitchen table. "Sit down. I'll serve."

"This is a surprise," Carole said. "You haven't cooked a meal since before Suzie was born and I was suffering from morning sickness."

"Enjoy." Jack ignored her snide remark and put a stack of waffles on the table, poured coffee for himself and Carole, orange juice for Suzie, and sat down across from his daughter.

Suzie drew a long breath, and sighed. "Mom, please don't be hurt, but I don't want you to go to school with me. I'm a senior now, and able to enroll myself."

Carole was hurt. She was also angry. "I have enrolled you in school since the first grade."

"I know that Mom, and for the last three years, I have been embarrassed by your presence."

"Why didn't you say something before now?"

Jack intruded into the conversation as if this concerned him. "She didn't want to hurt you."

A car horn sounded outside.

With swift surety, Suzie stood, drank the last of her orange juice, brushed Carole cheeks with her lips, threw a kiss in her dad's direction, grabbed her purse, and ran for the door.

Carole called after her, "Suzanne Marie Garner, come back here."

The answer was the slamming of the front door. She turned to face Jack. "This is your fault."

ASKING FOR A MIRACLE

"I agree. I should have stepped in long ago and put a stop to you micro-managing every phase of Suzanne's life. I didn't want to rock the boat." His eyes were gray pools of sadness. "Since the boat has capsized, I don't know if it can be up-righted again. For that I am sorry, but I'm not sorry enough to sit by and let you stunt Suzanne's emotional growth by being so controlling."

"I am not a bad mother." Carole took a gulp of coffee. It was cold. "Stop calling Suzie Suzanne."

"Suzanne doesn't want to be Suzie anymore. She asked to be called by her complete name."

"You are a perfect father?" Carole sneered, and then added, "I will call my daughter by any name I choose." There was an element of truth in Jack's accusation. Her anger drained away. "The coffee is cold." She looked at the kitchen wall clock. "You are going to be late for work."

"I'm staying right here." He slapped the table with his hand. "Until you agree to talk to me."

She knew Jack. He was as stubborn as a Missouri mule. "I'll make more coffee."

"And then we can talk?" He eyed her cautiously. "With no holds barred and nothing off-limits?"

"I have household chores to do. After that, we can talk." She stood and moved toward the stove.

Chapter Eight

September 3, 1974, Tuesday Afternoon

Carole lingered, finding extra chores to do. Jack suspected she was killing time, postponing the inevitable as long as possible.

He took command of the situation by making sandwiches for lunch, and fetching her from the bathroom where he found her scrubbing the shower. "Lunch is ready."

"I still—" Carole put her hand over her mouth and giggled as she followed him from the bathroom into the kitchen.

"What's so funny?" How could she laugh when their present was in turmoil and their future so uncertain?

"You are, in that frilly apron." Carole followed him down the hall and into the kitchen.

He looked down at the fancy gingham apron he wore and grinned. "I hope you like tuna sandwiches. Sit down. Lunch is ready."

They ate in edgy silence.

After a night of tossing and turning, Jack had reached the conclusion that his long-ago affair was not the only problem in their marriage. It was merely the catalyst that brought so many other obstacles into focus. Carole ate her sandwich, drank her tea, and wiped her mouth with a paper napkin. "You want to talk? I'm listening."

Where should he begin? The answer was clear. At the beginning. "Do you remember the night I proposed to you?"

"Like it was yesterday. Why do you ask?"

"I should have taken you to a fancy restaurant, got down on my knees, and spoken pretty words of love. Instead, I sat beside you on Aunt Effie's couch, put one arm around your shoulder, and said 'Will you marry me?' Was that proposal a disappointment to you?"

"You're not the romantic type. I knew it then. I know it now." She raked crumbs from the table into her hand and dumped them into her plate.

"That's not what I asked." He waited, desperate to know and dreading to hear.

She answered with a question of her own. "Was our wedding night a disappointment to you? Did it make a difference in how you thought of me?"

It was, and it did. He was hesitant to say so. "I assumed you were a passionate woman. Your response was...not what I expected."

"My response was no response at all. Afterward, I tried to explain. You wouldn't listen."

He had refused to listen to what she had to say. What man wants to hear he is a failure as a lover? They never spoke of it after that. "I wondered why you were so cold."

"I tried to tell you. I wasn't cold. I was scared. Aunt Effie never spoke to me about marriage until two days before our wedding. I was already a nervous wreck. Her 'birds and bees' explanation of marital relations didn't help." She wiped tears from her cheeks. "Looking back, I can understand why."

"I should have been more gentle. I never dreamed you were a virgin. After that, things improved."

"But they were not all right, not for a long time."

He'd been wrong not to hear her explanation. He knew that now. Why didn't he let her explain? His fear of being an inadequate lover? He nodded to himself, knowing that was the truth.

"Before you were drafted, we talked about divorce. Yet you never mentioned it in your letters, or after you came home." She bowed her head and stared at her plate.

He wanted to tell her he was a basket case when he returned from that place, and all that had happened there. He needed her to help him find his way back to the place he was when he was drafted. Had he admitted that, she might have walked out on him then and there. "Why didn't *you* mention it?"

"You were an emotional wreck when you came home. I couldn't bring up something as wrenching as divorce at a time like that."

Had she stayed with him out of pity? "Then we lost our newborn son." Carole swallowed before adding, "Two years later Suzie came along." She had stopped crying. Tears still dimmed the blue of her eyes. "We have never had much of a marriage, have we?"

Those words brought an unexpected stab of pain. "Why did you say yes to my proposal?"

"I wanted a home and children, and I loved you." She clasped her hands together, laid them in her lap, and stared down at them. "Why did you ask me?"

"I was twenty-eight years old. I wanted to get away from my mother constantly intruding into my life. I thought having a wife and a home would do that." That was a poor excuse for making a life-long commitment. "I loved you, too."

Carole looked him squarely in the eye. "I was a disappointment to you from the very beginning. You had a serious affair in Korea. Either of us placing blame would be like the pot calling the kettle black. Do you want a divorce?"

Jack thought for a long time, before saying, "No, never. Do you?"

She shook her head. "No, not if we can repair our marriage."

How did they go about repairing something that had been broken from the beginning? "Where do we start?"

"I thought about our situation most of last night," Carole replied. "We need to be apart for a while. Maybe it will give us each a new perspective. I am moving to Aunt Effie's house. I want to find out more about my father, and about Aunt Effie. I lived with her all my life, and I really never knew her. Are you agreeable to that arrangement?"

"Do you think that's the answer?" He didn't want her to go. He needed her here, beside him. *Why didn't I know that before now?*

BILLIE HOUSTON

"I have to go. Since Aunt Effie's death my life has become a tangled muddle of confusion."

"Running away won't help. What about Suzanne?"

"She will come with me." Carole picked up her paper napkin, rolled it into a ball, and pitched it on the table.

"She will have to change schools. I doubt she will want to do that." He spoke with grim determination. "The choice is Suzanne's. That's the only way I will agree to such an arrangement."

Carole's expression hardened. "Okay, I agree, but don't be surprised when Suzie chooses to come with me."

Chapter Nine

September 18, 1974, Wednesday Afternoon
Carole closed the second ledger, pushed her chair back from the desk, and sighed. Over the last two weeks she had read every word in Aunt Effie's ledgers, not once, but twice. The second time she took numerous notes. So many questions, but where did she start looking for answers? She spent her spare time talking with Suzie on the telephone, advising her how to arrange with her school to make her transfer to another district speedy and simple. Despite all the things she felt pressed to do, she was lonely, especially in the evenings. She missed her daughter. She missed Jack too, even though she was hesitant to admit that, even to herself.
The ringing of the telephone cut through her wandering thoughts. She ran to answer it. Suzie promised to call this evening. Maybe she decided to call early. She answered with a hopeful, "Hello."
Suzie's young voice sounded in her ear. "Mom, hello."
"Have you settled things at school? When will you be moving in with me?"
"I'm not coming to live there. I'm staying here, with Dad. He needs me, and I don't want to leave Woodrow Wilson High."
The words sent shock waves through Carole as they echoed in her head like a death knell. *Take it easy. Don't lose your temper.* "Your place is here, with me. A girl your age needs her mother."
That belligerent tone she knew so well slipped into Suzie's voice. "Mom, why don't you come home? Dad and I both miss you."
"It's too complicated to explain."
"Stop treating me like a child. I am an adult, and I have a right to know why my mother left my dad."

Carole knew she wouldn't understand, at least not fully. Is that what frightened her? She took a deep breath and bit back a caustic reply. "Have you talked to Dad?" Had Jack set about to deliberately turn her child against her? Surely not. Yet that little whisper of doubt wouldn't go away.

"I talk to Daddy every day. He listens to me and considers my opinions." A knock on the door was a welcome interruption. "I have a visitor. I'll call you after school tomorrow." Carole put the receiver on its hook, and hurried toward the front door.

She swung it open to see Midge standing on the front porch. She unhooked the screen and held it open. "Where have you been? I've been trying to get in touch with you for two weeks."

Midge stepped inside and closed the screen. "Elbert and I went camping up in Big Bend."

"Come inside. I'll make some iced tea. I have some questions to ask you. Like why would you go camping when you hate the outdoors?"

"Forget the tea." Midge plopped down on the couch. "I have some questions for you too. Like what are you doing living in Aunt Effie's house?"

Carole sat on the arm of the overstuffed chair across from Midge, uncomfortable, and not knowing why. "Jack and I are separated."

"Since when?"

"Since Labor Day." She asked again, this time more pointedly. "What brought about your sudden love for camping?"

"I don't love camping. I did it to please Elbert. He's the one who loves camping."

It was not like Midge to put someone else's desires above her own. "You never took up any of your other husbands' hobbies."

"Maybe if I had, I wouldn't be starting on husband number four. This may be my last chance at marriage. I want it to be a happy one this time around." She took a long breath. "Did you say something about tea?"

ASKING FOR A MIRACLE

They went to the kitchen where Carole made a pitcher of tea, and filled two tall glasses with ice cubes.

Midge sat at Aunt Effie's prized kitchen table. "Tell me what happened between you and Jack."

"It's complicated."

"Nothing is complicated unless you choose to make it that way."

"Jack had an affair while he was in Korea." Carole poured tea, put the two glasses on the table, and sat across from Midge. "It was serious. The woman was Korean. Her name was Chong Sun. They had a child. She died in childbirth. A few days later, the child died too. Jack never breathed a word of this to me. Twenty-one years later, at a Texas Korean War Veterans' Convention, one of his buddies let it slip." She sat back and took a sip of tea. She was weary of all the heartache and confusion in her life.

"Is that all?"

"Isn't that enough?" Carole needed someone to understand her dilemma, and offer sympathy. Obviously that someone was not her oldest and best friend.

"No, it's not," Midge snapped. "You have, or at least you had, a man who came home every day after work. He provided for you. He is a good father. Do you know what a rare combination that is?"

"Jack was unfaithful to me." Carole took a gulp of tea to ease the tightness in her throat.

Midge reached across the table and caught both of Carole's hands in hers. "Listen to me old friend, and listen well. You are a fool if you don't patch up things with Jack."

"There's something else," Carole admitted, even though it pained her to do so. Midge's words jarred her balance. Had she made a mistake?

"Do you want to tell me?"

"Not really, but I think I need to. Maybe I should have told someone a long time ago. When I married Jack, I was a virgin. I knew nothing about men or marriage. Two or three days before the ceremony Aunt

43

Effie gave me her version of what to expect on my wedding night. Her belated explanation about marital relations fueled the fears I already harbored. The first night of our honeymoon was a big disappointment to both of us."

"Is that all?" Midge squeezed Carole's hands before letting go. "That's no big deal."

"It was to Jack. He was, to say the least, disappointed."

"What did he say?"

"Not much." As painful as it was to dredge up the past, Carole continued. "Afterward, he turned away from me, and said something about being inadequate. I didn't answer. He went to the bathroom and stayed a long time. When he came back, I pretended to be asleep. We never spoke of it again, until the day I left to come and live here, but it affected our marriage."

"Why didn't you talk to each other and try to work things out?" Midge stirred her tea and waited for an answer.

"I tried. Jack refused to respond. Then he went off to war. Things were different when he came back. He was different, too. I thought why stir up trouble at this late date? I pushed it to the back of my mind. Eventually we both forgot it."

"Hooey." Midge did have a way of putting things into perspective. "Neither of you ever forgot it." She snapped her fingers. "Talk to Pastor Norman about this. He can help you."

"I couldn't do that." Carole sat in her chair, and gripped the edge of the table. "Talk to my pastor about something so intimate? I would die of embarrassment."

Midge, blunt as always, replied, "You'd better get some help from somewhere if you want to keep your husband."

Chapter Ten

October 12, 1974, Saturday Morning

Jack woke suddenly and turned over, expecting to see Carole sleeping beside him. She wasn't there. Would she ever lie beside him again? He was beginning to wonder. She left over a month ago. He had heard nothing from her since. The first two weeks she was gone, she called Suzanne every day. After Suzanne made the choice to stay with him, she had been as silent as a tomb.

He should have called her long ago. The thought that she had packed up and left him, possibly for good, was beyond painful. She took most of her things. Still, he was reluctant to initiate a dialogue. If she wanted to talk, she would have to make the first move.

He had spent the last few weeks getting to know the grown-up version of his daughter. She proved to be a delight—bright, personable, and so in need of a parent's interest and acceptance. Today she would be going with him to his office. When he offered her the job of filing papers while he caught up on bookwork, she jumped at the chance.

He got out of bed and dressed. He was beginning to see Carole's point about spending more time with his family. When he came downstairs Suzanne sat on the couch, waiting for him.

She smiled when she saw him. "Good morning, Daddy. I would have cooked breakfast if I knew how to cook. We could have cold cereal, but we don't have any milk. I would have made coffee, but I'm not sure how. I have a lot to learn if I'm going to take proper care of you."

Her words, so earnestly spoken, moved Jack. "I'm the one who is supposed to be taking care of you. How about we go to some fast-food place for breakfast?" He moved toward the front door.

BILLIE HOUSTON

Suzanne jumped to her feet. "I know just the place. Cindy and I eat there often. Mom calls it a greasy spoon." She asked, as she followed Jack onto the front porch, "Do you think Mom will ever come home?"

His first impulse was to assure his daughter that her mother would come home, and soon. Second thoughts gave him pause. He had promised to treat her as an adult. "I don't know, sweetie. I honestly don't know."

Suzanne was usually a regular chatterbox. As they drove to breakfast, she was strangely quiet. Jack respected her silence. Nonetheless, he wondered what her thoughts were and why she chose not to share them.

They were inside The Burger Bar, had placed their order, and were seated before she broke her self-imposed quiet. "I have to ask you a question. If you don't want to tell me, I will try to understand, but I need to know."

A teenage waiter appeared carrying a loaded tray. "Who gets the pancakes and bacon?"

"I do." Suzanne raised her hand.

He set the pancakes before her, along with a pitcher of syrup. "Enjoy." He put the bacon and eggs before Jack. "Would you like more coffee, sir?"

"Later." Jack picked up his plastic knife and spread butter over his biscuits. As the waiter walked away, he said, "You wanted to ask me a question. Fire away."

"Why is Mom mad at you?" Suzanne poured a liberal amount of syrup over her pancakes.

He sat staring at her in stunned silence. Her words hit him with the force of a body blow.

"Please tell me. I have a right to know and I'm old enough to understand."

Jack doubted she was. She might hate him, and just when he was beginning to establish a relationship with her.

ASKING FOR A MIRACLE

"You promised to treat me like an adult."

"What happened doesn't say much for me as a husband. It happened a long time ago." Sooner or later she would find out, now that the cat was out of the bag. He drew in a long breath. "This is not something any father would want to tell his daughter, but you deserve the truth. It happened before you were born. You know I fought in the Korean War."

*****

October 12, 1974
Saturday Afternoon

Carole was reading a letter for the third time when she heard a car pull into her driveway. She pushed the letter back into the envelope and hurried to open the front door.

Otis closed the door to his pickup. She stepped onto the front porch. *What now?*

He waved as he came up the front steps. "I was in the neighborhood so I thought I'd stop by."

"Since when did you start working on Saturday afternoons?" She went inside and held the door open for him.

"Since your neighbor down the street decided she wants the paneling in her den put up yesterday." He followed her into the living room.

"Sit down." Carole pointed toward a chair. Otis did small carpentry and repair jobs. Carole suspected he didn't need the income. He did need to have something to occupy his time, especially after he lost his wife, Nari, to breast cancer almost five years ago. "Would you like a glass of iced tea?"

"Yes, ma'am."

Carole headed for the kitchen. Otis followed her, and sat down at the kitchen table.

"Make yourself at home." Carole took a pitcher from the refrigerator and poured them each a glass. She put one before Otis and sat down across from him. "How have you been? Are your tomato vines bearing yet?"

"I didn't come here to pass pleasantries." He moved his glass around on the table, leaving little wet circles. "I came to tell you to get back home where you belong."

"Butt out, Otis. This is none of your business." *How dare he be so nosey and so blunt?*

"Anything that hurts Jack is my business. He's hurting now like I never saw him hurt before."

"What did Jack tell you?" Carole's appetite for tea vanished. She pushed her glass from her.

"He didn't tell me anything. He didn't have to. I've known the man for over twenty years. I can read him like a book. I suspect this has something to do with what happened in Korea with Chong Sun?"

Carole glared at him and refused to answer.

Several seconds ticked by before Otis said, "What happened to Jack in Korea is none of your business."

His bluntness she could overlook. His rudeness she would not tolerate. "Since when is a man's infidelity not his wife's business?"

Otis lowered his voice and pleaded with her. "Please, try to understand—"

"I've heard it all before." Carole jumped to her feet. "You were killing and being killed. Life was cheap. You were far from home and lonely. Death lurked around every corner—"

"You've heard it, but you didn't live it." He stood, and pushed his chair under the table. "I'm sorry if I offended you. I have to go now." He took long strides toward the front door.

Carole followed him, almost stepping on his heels. "I'm sorry too." *What must I be thinking to lose my temper that way?* "I know your intentions are the best."

ASKING FOR A MIRACLE

At the door Otis stopped, lifted his ball cap from his head with one hand and raked his fingers through his hair with the other. "Think about what I said." He left, closing the door behind him.

Carole went back to her desk and retrieved the letter she got this morning. It was the second answer she had received to one of the many ads she'd placed in newspapers in and around the little city of Cedar Gap, Texas. The first letter was no help at all. This one seemed more promising. She unfolded it, laid it on her desk, and read:

> Dear Carole Garner,
>
> I saw your ad in the Cedar Gap Sentinel. I think I may be one of the Douds you are searching for. My mother was a Doud before she married Anderson Whitley. She had a sister named Mary Agnes. We visited her and Uncle Tom often when I was a little girl. I remember they had a little girl about my age.
>
> I am ninety-two years old and live in an assisted living apartment in Cedar Gap. The name of the place is Freedom Acres. I no longer travel, but I would welcome a visit from you.
>
> Sincerely,
>
> Mary Beth Whitley

Carole slipped the letter back into its envelope. Was there a chance Mary Beth Whitley was Aunt Effie's cousin? There was one sure way to find out. She would go to Cedar Gap tomorrow. Since it was a four-hour drive, she would have to stay overnight and come home Monday.

Chapter Eleven

October 13, 1974, Sunday Morning

Jack lay in his bed and stared at the ceiling. Was telling Suzanne about him and Chong Sun a mistake? She listened as he told her the truth, as he knew it. Afterward, she sat across from him and stared, but said nothing. When she did speak, it was to change the subject.

"Do you think I could work for you next summer before I go off to college?"

"I think that's a great idea." *She's still speaking to me. That's a plus.*

Later, at the office, Jack gave her instructions before sitting down at his desk and going to work.

Three hours passed. Suzanne finished her task and came to sit in a chair near his desk.

"I straightened your files. They were a mess."

"Thank you." He would probably catch what-for from Bridget tomorrow. It wouldn't be the first time in the last fifteen years his secretary was unhappy with him.

"Daddy?"

"Yes?" Jack completed his last task and closed the manila folder before him.

"Why did you decide to become the owner of a hardware store?"

"I didn't. Fate decided for me." He leaned back in his chair and rolled it until he faced her. "I wanted to be an engineer. Grandpa Garner was diagnosed with cancer the summer between my junior and senior years at UT. The store belonged to him, but he was too sick to run it. His medical bills were astronomical. There was no money for college. Somebody had to step in and run the store." He shrugged. "That

somebody was me. I never got around to going back to school. That's how I ended up in the hardware business."
"I didn't know that." Suzanne leaned forward and smiled. "I feel as if I'm just getting to know you, and you've been my dad all my life."
"I should hope so." Jack stood. "Let's eat some lunch, and then find a grocery store."

*****

"Daddy."
Suzanne calling from downstairs pulled him from his wool-gathering. "Come to breakfast. Uncle Otis is here. He made coffee. There's milk and cereal."
Jack came downstairs and into the dining room. Otis sat at the table nursing a cup of coffee. "Hi, buddy. How's it going?" Jack sat down.
Suzanne put a cup of coffee in front of him. "I can make toast to go with your cereal."
"No thanks, sweetie. I'm fine."
"I'll take some of that toast." Otis held up two fingers. "With lots of butter."
"Coming up." ′Suzanne disappeared into the kitchen.
She was scarcely out of sight when Otis opened up. "I dropped by Aunt Effie's house yesterday."
Otis meant well, but he could be a pain at times "Stay out of this, Otis. This is between Carole and me. We will work things out eventually."
"Not if all you do is sit and wait for it to happen. Go see her. Try to talk some sense into her head."
"It's not a sense matter. It's a heart matter."
Suzanne came from the kitchen with four slices of toast, slightly burned, and slathered with butter. She set the plate on the table. "I made toast for you too, Daddy. It burned a little. I scraped it though."
"It looks delicious." Jack lifted a slice to his mouth and took a bite.
Otis followed suit. "Girl, this is good eating."

ASKING FOR A MIRACLE

The telephone rang. Suzanne raced to answer it.

The moment she was out of hearing distance, Otis began again. "Did you know Carole put ads in all the newspapers in and around the little town where Aunt Effie was born? She's looking for members of the Doud family. Why would she do that?"

"Did she tell you that's what she did?" This was news to Jack.

"No, shoot no. She's not very friendly toward me at the moment."

Suzanne reappeared. "That was Grandma. She says for you to stay put. She will be over soon. She wants to talk to you."

"Did she say what she wanted?" As if he didn't know.

"She didn't say." Suzanne made for the stairs. "I'm going to Cindy's. I'll be home before five."

"Be careful." Jack didn't blame her for bailing. He would escape, too, if he could.

"I gotta go too." Otis crammed half a piece of toast in his mouth. "So long."

"Just a minute, friend. You're staying right here until you explain how you found out about Carole's ads."

"I can't betray a confidence."

"Somebody told you to look for ads." Who would do that, and why?

"It was more of a hint." Otis reached for another slice of toast. He took a bite and chewed. "I can give you a hint. Who is Carole's best friend?"

"Midge told you?" Disbelief jarred Jack. "She hates my guts, and she's not overly fond of you. Why would she tell you, of all people, something like that?"

Otis shrugged. "She didn't say, but I got the idea that she'd like to see you and Carole back together."

"Since when has Midge been in my corner and not Carole's? When and where did you see her?"

"She called me on the phone Saturday night."

The doorbell rang. Otis jumped to his feet and took off for the back door like he was shot from a cannon. "See you later."

BILLIE HOUSTON

*****

October 13, 1974
Sunday Afternoon

Carole's nerves danced a jig down her backbone. She found apartment 127, where Mary Beth Whitley's name was enclosed in a plaque by the door. She knocked and waited.

It opened slowly at first, and then swung wide. The woman on the other side was skinny and short in stature. Her silver-gray hair was twisted into a knot atop her head. She stood erect. Her blue-veined hands clutched the cane she held in front of her. "My dear, you must be lost. Whom are you searching for?"

"Mary Beth Whitley." A thought she had never before considered entered Carole's mind. Suppose Mary Beth Whitley was not of sound mind? "Do you know where I can find her?"

"You have found her." The old woman stepped back. "You must be Carole Garner. Please come inside."

Carole breathed a sigh of relief as she stepped into a cozy sitting area and looked around at the furnishings. "I like your room, especially your Tiffany lamps." She moved a pillow, and sat on one end of the couch. "Thank you for seeing me, Mrs. Whitley."

"The lamps are heirlooms and the name is Miss Whitley, but since we seem to be related, call me Mary Beth."

"Are we related? Are you sure?"

"Not absolutely, but I have pictures of my mother and her sisters. I had my niece bring them to me after I wrote you. There's an album in the top drawer of the chest in my sleeping area. Will you fetch it and bring it to me, dear?"

Carole hurried to do Mary Beth's bidding. She came back into the sitting area to find Mary Beth rested on the other end of the couch.

ASKING FOR A MIRACLE

Carole could hardly contain her excitement. Mary Beth had referred to her as her niece. It was nice to have family. Distant though they may be, they were still family.

Mary Beth turned on one of the Tiffany lamps. Its soft glow cast a halo of light around them. She laid the album in Carole's lap. "Let's see what we can find."

The album was old, frayed at the corners, and smelled faintly of cedar. Carole turned to the first page. Some of the pictures were yellow with age. Others were faded to near white.

Mary Beth pointed to a photo of three young women dressed in turn-of-the-century styles. "That's me and my two sisters. They are both gone now." She rubbed her fingers across the picture. "I miss them."

"You were all very attractive." This was going to take longer than she thought. Carole turned to the next page. It was then that she saw it, a picture of a very young Aunt Effie seated in a chair with her hands folded in her lap. She wore a long black skirt, a Gibson-girl blouse, and high-button shoes. Written beneath in flowing script were the words Mary Elizabeth Effington age fourteen. "Who is this?"

Mary Beth leaned forward and narrowed her gaze. "That's my cousin. She's two years older than I am. Our names are almost the same. Aunt Agnes was unhappy when Mama named me Mary Beth. Mama said she'd get over her mad, and she did, but it took some time."

At this rate I'll be here until midnight. "Is Mary Elizabeth still alive?"

"It's strange you should ask." Mary Beth removed her glasses, wiped them on her dress tail, and set them back on her nose. "I don't know all the details, but I will be happy to tell you what I do know. Much of it is hearsay, mind you, and it happened a long time ago. It was all very hush-hush."

"I understand." *Get on with it.*

"Would you like something to drink, dear?"

"No, thank you."

BILLIE HOUSTON

"I would." Mary Beth nodded toward her sleeping area. "There's a tiny refrigerator on my chest. Would you fetch me a strawberry soda? Bring one for yourself, too. I have much to tell you."

Chapter Twelve

October 13, 1974, Sunday Morning
Clarissa sat straight and stiff on the edge of the living room couch, folded her hands in her lap, and looked around the room. "Where is Suzie?"
"She's out." Jack slid into his easy chair and tried to relax.
"I can see that." His mother huffed out an irritated breath.
"She's at Cindy's."
"That's convenient." Clarissa leaned back, and uncrossed her ankles. "I worry about our younger generation. Do you know how many nuclear explosions have been set off around the world since the middle of August?" Before Jack could respond she answered her own question. "Five that we know about and heaven only knows how many that were never mentioned to the public." She splayed her hand across her bosom. "What kind of a contaminated world are we leaving for our children and grandchildren?"
"Not a very good—"
Clarissa interrupted and was off again. "My ladies club is circulating a petition to send to our senator. We are demanding he introduce a bill that places a worldwide ban on nuclear testing."
So, this was his mother's latest cause to champion. He guessed it was better than demanding all the *indecent* books be taken from the public library and destroyed.
"We have stated to Mr. Bentsen, up front, that even though we are all staunch Democrats, we will not vote for him if he ignores our demands." She waved one hand in a dismissive manner. "Be that as it may, that's not what I came to talk to you about."

So, she knew about Carole moving out. Jack braced himself for his mother's next tirade. "It's only temporary."

"Oh. Is it?" Clarissa raised one well-arched eyebrow. "Then explain to me why Stephen came yesterday to move the last of his things out of Margie's house? My daughter is devastated."

"Steve? Margie's husband? Obviously, we aren't on the same page. I thought—never mind what I thought. Don't worry about Steve leaving. He will come back, he always does."

"Not this time, at least not without someone showing him the error of his ways. You must talk to him. He respects you. He will listen to what you have to say. Tell him marriage is forever. He can't just walk away from Margie."

Jack laughed, a bitter, caustic guffaw that echoed across the room. "Carole has left me, Mother, in case you didn't know. Who am I to go around handing out marital advice?"

"I know." Clarissa sighed before adding, "In your case, it's different."

He would never understand his mother's convoluted logic. "I fail to see that difference."

"Margie wants to come home and live with me. I told her that was not possible, but she says she's coming anyway."

The light dawned. Mother wanted Steve to reunite with Margie for purely selfish reasons. "Will you turn her out when she arrives?"

"Maybe I won't have to. Maybe." Clarissa paused and took a deep breath. "Maybe Margie can come here and live with you for a while. Now that Carole is gone, you need a housekeeper. Who better than your own flesh and blood?"

"Margie is not a child." Jack was appalled at such a suggestion. "She can sell her house, find an apartment, and live alone."

"Don't you think I suggested that?" Clarissa's voice rose in indignation. "She flatly refuses."

"She can't come here," Jack declared. "That's final. It looks like you are stuck with providing shelter for your child."

ASKING FOR A MIRACLE

Clarissa stood. "I will do no such thing. If her own brother won't take her in, she's on her own." She marched, with head held high, toward the door.

Jack knew Clarissa Arabella Wentworth Garner. She meant every word she said. "Come back and sit down. We will work out something."

*****

Carole returned with the sodas and gave one to Mary Beth before sitting in a chair and scooting it near the old lady. She took a long drink of her soda, and waited.

After taking a sip of her drink, Mary Beth began to speak. "Mother always said the Doud sisters' children got their brains from the Doud side of the family. Lizzie was the smartest of us all."

"When you say Lizzie, do you mean Mary Elizabeth, your cousin who was two years your senior?" Carole wanted to make sure they were speaking of the same person.

"Of course I am. There were so many Marys in the family, and so many Elizabeths. We had to do something to distinguish among them. Mama always said it was Aunt Agnes' fault, all that confusion. Aunt Agnes was always quick to answer that Mama knew how many Marys and how many Elizabeths there were in the family before she named me. They often had words over it. Grandma's name was Elizabeth too. I remember once—"

"You were telling me about your cousin, Mary Elizabeth."

"Was I? Oh yes. Where was I?"

"You said she was very intelligent." Carole took another sip of her soda, and waited.

"I said she was smart," Mary Elizabeth spoke emphatically, "and she was. She wanted to go to college, but of course, that was out of the question in those days. She did go to Miss Ipha Osborne's Secretarial School for Women, and graduated at the top of her class. After that, she got a job as a bookkeeper at J. D. Henderson's cotton gin. She was good at what she did. J. D. himself said she was the best bookkeeper he ever had. She worked there ten years and then he fired her when cotton prices dropped to fifteen dollars a bale. He kept the lazy lout he'd hired as office manager. He explained that he kept the man because he had a family to support."

"That's terrible." Poor mother.

"He got his comeuppance," Mary Beth declared, and then gave a nod of her head. "That office manager didn't know a credit from a debit. That was when J. D. came looking for Lizzie. He was ready to beg her to come back and work for him. He even planned to give her a raise."

"Did she go back to work for him? I hope she told him what he could do with his raise."

"She was gone by then." Mary Beth put her soda bottle on the table beside the couch arm. "She found a job that paid her almost twice what J. D. was going to offer."

"Where did she go?" Carole's body tingled with excitement.

"She went to Dallas to work for some firm that manufactured electrical household appliance, things like irons, toasters, and radios. It was a new business. I can't recall the name of the company."

"Try, please try to remember." My first real clue.

"I don't remember as well as I used to." Mary Beth rubbed her hand across her forehead. "I'm not good with dates. I never was."

"Can you give me an approximate date?" Perspiration broke out above Carole's upper lip.

The old woman's parchment brow wrinkled into a frown. She bowed her head, drummed her fingers on the couch arm and mumbled under her breath. Suddenly she raised her head. "The best I can calculate it was somewhere around nineteen twenty or nineteen-twenty-one."

By knowing more, she knew less. "Did you visit her there? Did she come back often to visit her family?"

"She didn't come back at all. After a while she stopped writing to me." Mary Beth shook her head from side to side. "As the years slid by, Aunt Agnes and Uncle Tom stopped talking about her."

Was this old woman lying? Carole suspected she might be omitting important details. Maybe she couldn't remember. How reliable was this information? "Did Lizzie have siblings?"

"She had one sister, Hattie May, Hattie died in nineteen twenty-seven, I think. Maybe it was nineteen twenty-eight. Aunt Agnes and Uncle Tom both died soon after." Mary Beth leaned her head against the back of the couch. "It was all so sad. Please don't ask me any more questions. I am growing weary of remembering."

"One other thing, and then I will go. What was the name of the man in Dallas that employed Lizzie?"

Mary Beth lifted her head. "I can't remember. Why are you so interested in Lizzie?"

"I will explain it all later. For now, you must rest, and I must go." Carole stood and walked toward the door.

Mary Beth called after her, "Do you promise to visit me again?"

"I promise. Rest now."

Chapter Thirteen

October 25, 1974, Friday Afternoon
Jack set the three suitcases he carried on the foyer floor. He had the feeling he would live to regret this.
Margie followed behind carrying a smaller suitcase and a duffel bag. "Where do I put these?"
"Put them here for now. Later we will take them up to the guest room." He went into the living room.
Margie followed him. "Where is Suzie?"
"I don't know." Jack sat on the couch and patted the cushion beside him. "Sit down. I have some things to say to you."
"Are you going to yell at me?" She sat. "How can you not know where Suzie is?"
"I am not going to yell at you, although I would like to. I am going to lay down a few rules."
"Like what?" She twisted to stare at him. "You sound like Mother, always telling me what to do."
"Will you shut up and listen?" Jack yelled. His sister would try the patience of a saint.
"You are yelling at me. You said you wouldn't." A tear slid down Margie's cheek.
"I'm sorry." Jack lowered his voice. A cramp knotted his stomach. "I want you to know we have rules around here, and everyone is expected to abide by them." He drew a deep breath, and was set to say more.
"Don't make me wash dishes or windows, please." She pulled a couch pillow into her embrace and held it against her middle.
"We have a dishwasher. I hire a window washer every six months." *I now have two teenagers on my hands. One is seventeen and one is forty-seven.*

"Rule one is you are responsible for yourself, your clothes, and your meals, and if you make a mess, you clean it up. Rule two is you must call your niece by her name. It's Suzanne. Don't call her Suzie ever again. Rule three is don't go into Suzanne's room, and under no circumstances will you ever use her Princess phone."

Margie blinked back tears. "I thought you were going to throw me out."

Jack wavered between sympathy and disgust. Sympathy won. "Let's get your things up to your room."

It took a while to get Margie settled in the guest room. By the time the job was completed Jack was exhausted and out-of-sorts. He headed for the door hoping to escape.

"There's one other thing I have to tell you," Margie called after him. "Steve quit his job at the hardware store."

"When did this happen?" Jack stopped and turned to face her. He knew nothing about Steve's resignation. There must be some mistake.

"He said he was handing in his resignation this afternoon." Margie looked around the room. "Where is my Princess telephone?"

Steve managed the automotive center of the store. He was indispensable. Jack had to find him and stop him from leaving. "I have to go now."

"You didn't answer my question." Margie scowled. "Where is my Princess telephone?"

"There is no telephone in this room." He turned to go. "I'll see you later. See if you can make dinner for the three of us. Have it ready around six."

"We can have one installed. Will scrambled eggs be okay for dinner?"

"You are not a 'we' in this house. You are a guest. If you wish to make a call, go downstairs. Forget dinner. I'll stop by the deli." If he lingered around, quarreling with Margie, he'd miss Steve. "Goodbye."

Marge's carping complaints followed him down the stairs. He went through the front door, got into his car, started it, and then raced for the hardware store.

ASKING FOR A MIRACLE

*****

Had Carole's searching all been in vain? Just when she despaired of ever finding anything about appliance companies in Dallas, the county librarian called her on the phone.

"Carole dear, I think I have found information relating to your search for appliance companies in the Dallas area in the nineteen twenties. It's in an old nineteen twenty-six obituary column in a Dallas newspaper. One David Duncan was electrocuted in a work-related accident. He was employed by the Always Able Appliance Company."

Carole's heart fluttered. "Read it to me."

"It's rather long, dear. I don't have time. I put the microfiche roll behind my desk. I'm saving it for you. Bye now."

Carole put on her shoes, grabbed her handbag and a sweater, and ran for her car. She was pulling into the library parking lot before she realized she wore no makeup and her hair was a mess. *I can't be bothered about so trivial a matter as my appearance at a time like this.* She got out of her car, slammed the door, and ran for the library entrance.

She opened the door and collided with Pastor Norman. He was a tall, middle-aged man, and solidly built. The impact jarred her back on her heels.

The first words out his mouth were, "We have been missing you at church. I pray all is well with you and Jack, and Suzanne."

"Yes, I –" Heat crept into her cheeks. She was blushing. *Not here, not now.* "I came to look at an obituary Miss Dilsby is saving for me." *Why in heaven's name did I say that?*

"It must be terribly important. I can see you are in a hurry. See you in church." He pushed through the library doors, and was gone.

Carole got in line and waited as two giggling girls checked out books. They moved away from the desk. She greeted Miss Dilsby. "Good afternoon."

"I didn't expect you so soon." Miss Dilsby reached under the counter and retrieved a square box. "This is a microfiche tape of The Dallas Morning Star News from 1920 through 1929. Do you know how to use the machine?"
"What machine?"
"The machine that allows you to read what's on the tape." Miss Dilsby came from behind her desk and motioned for Carole to follow her. "Come along, I'll show you."
Carole put the tape on a reel with a crank mounted on the side of a box-like creation with a screen in front. "It may take you a while to locate what you are looking for. Good luck."
She sat in front of the machine and turned the crank. Carole smiled as the archaic equipment chugged and groaned, making several spins. She spent the next thirty minutes learning to cope with this metal monster's idiosyncrasies, and another hour and a half looking for David Duncan's obituary.
Miss Dilsby checked on her periodically, always with a few words of encouragement.
When she found the obituary, she wanted to shout. She didn't dare. She grabbed an envelope and pencil from her handbag so she could write down any pertinent information she found.

David Dewhurst Duncan. Born March 2, 1903
Son of Oliver P. Duncan and Martha Dewhurst Duncan
Siblings: Oliver P. Duncan, Jr. and Esther Ann Duncan

She reread the information she had just found before asking herself. *Was Oliver P. Duncan my father? If so, do I have living Duncan relatives?* A tap on the shoulder brought her back to reality. Miss Dilsby smiled down at her. "The library will close in fifteen minutes."
"What time is it?"
"Five-forty-five."

ASKING FOR A MIRACLE

Carole stood and pushed her chair under the desk. "Thank you, Miss Dilsby. You have been a tremendous help."
"I am glad I could be of assistance. Good-bye, dear." Miss Dilsby hurried to assist an old gentleman standing in front of the check-out desk.
Carole picked up her belongings and headed for the door. *Success at last.*

.

Chapter Fourteen

October 31, 1974, Thursday Afternoon

Jack came to a stop before Steve's office door, pulled it open and went inside. Steve sat behind his desk. He was a tall man with receding hairline, and a rugged build. At this moment, he looked every day of his fifty-five years.

"I was afraid I would miss you." Jack closed the door. "Margie tells me you are resigning from your job. Say that isn't true."

Steve pointed to a chair. "Would you like to sit down?" The pessimistic note in his deep voice was not a harbinger of good news.

"I would like you to say you are not quitting your job." Jack sat in the chair and stared at his brother-in-law. "Would a raise in pay change your mind?" He considered Steve a friend as well as an in-law. "I thought you liked being manager of the automotive department."

"I do. That's not the problem." Steve pushed back his office chair. "It's, well, I need some time to find myself. I'm going to Dallas to visit my son and daughter."

"You don't plan to take Margie with you?" That was a stupid question. Margie made no secret of her dislike of Steve's children by his first marriage.

"Margie and I are separated." Steve's eyes narrowed. "I think you knew that before you came in here."

"You will kiss and make up," Jack replied with more assurance than he felt.

"Not this time." Steve slashed his index finger across his throat. "I've had it up to here with that woman."

Like a bolt from the blue the truth hit Jack. "You're not ever coming back." He asked, as if he had every right to do so, "Do you love Margie?"

BILLIE HOUSTON

Anger flashed across Steve's rough-hewn features. "Not that it's any of your business, but yes, I do, very much. I love her but I can't live with her." He held up one hand to stop Jack from saying more. "You and I have skirted the subject of your sister—my wife—for years. I see no point in discussing her now."

"Carole has left me. I don't know if she will ever come back." The words slipped out before Jack could stop them.

"I don't believe it." Steve's jaw clenched. "What happened?"

"It's about something that happened a long time ago. Carole found out about it a few weeks back. She's living now in the house her Aunt Effie left her. I thought she would come home when Suzanne refused to move with her. She didn't. She's fixated now on—" Jack paused as he debated if he should continue. In for a penny, in for a pound. "Carole learned after Aunt Effie passed away that the woman she believed for all these years to be her great aunt was really her mother. Now she—"

Surprise brought Steve to a standing position. "Aunt Effie was Carole's mother?"

Jack nodded. "It's true. Now Carole can think of nothing but searching for any other relatives she may have. She wants to learn as much as she can about her father."

Steve sat back down, and asked, "You objected, and she left you? That doesn't sound like the level-headed Carole I know."

"It's not that simple. Carole left me because she learned that while I was in Korea, I had an affair with another woman. The woman died giving birth to our child. The child died too."

"I thought I had troubles." Steve ran his fingers through his hair. "Women. Your wife is a strait-laced confused woman, but she is a grown woman. My wife is a little girl emotionally. I thought when we married she would mature once I got her from under her mother's roof. I failed. After ten years, she's still Clarissa's little girl. She's gone back to live permanently with her mother. I can't take it anymore. I have to get away."

ASKING FOR A MIRACLE

Jack knew he had to be honest. "Mother refused to let Margie come home. She's staying with me."

Steve's face was a kaleidoscope of changing emotions "That—" He stopped. " Sorry Jack. I will come by this evening and take her home."

"That's the worst thing you could do." *Who am I to be handing out marital advice?* "My little sister needs to grow up. I have told her that with Carole away she will be shouldering some of the household duties."

Steve laughed. "Lots of luck. Margie can't cook. She never made a bed or washed a dish in her life."

"If she wants a roof over her head she will have to learn how to do both," Jack announced with finality.

"Would you turn her out into the street? What kind of a brother are you?" Steve struck his desktop with his fist. "She'd be lost and scared to death."

"I would never turn her out," Jack assured him, "but she doesn't know that."

"Be gentle with her." Tears were in Steve's eyes.

"I will, as gentle as I can be." *He really loves her.* Jack stood. "Will you stay on as manager of the automotive department until I can find someone to take your place?"

"I will stay so long as you take care of Margie."

That was blackmail, but Jack agreed. "It's a deal."

Jack's hand was on the doorknob when Steve called out to him. "Go see Carole. Talk to her. Ask her to come back to you. Beg a little if that's what it takes."

"I'll think about it." Jack hurried into the hall. The last thing he needed now was a lecture from some well-meaning, but misguided, in-law. He slammed the door behind him.

*****

November 4, 1974

BILLIE HOUSTON

Monday Morning

Carole parked her car and looked around. The sign over the door read Green Valley Home for Senior Citizens. This was the place. She didn't look forward to the task ahead of her.

Carole discovered the name Henry Benson while researching for information about her father. He was pallbearer at Oliver senior's funeral. She hired a detective to track down the man. This was her last hope of learning something personal about her father. She got out of the car and walked toward the front door of the Green Valley Home for senior citizens.

She went inside. A gum-chewing young woman with a Farrah Fawcett hairdo sat behind the reception desk reading a paperback novel. She looked up when Carole approached the desk.

"May I help you?"

"I'm looking for Mr. Henry Benson. I understand he's a resident here." Carole smiled.

"He's in the sun room." The young woman nodded toward the center hallway before she turned her attention back to her book.

Carole hesitated. "Do I need to sign in?"

Without looking up, the young woman shook her head. "No."

Carole took a tentative step, and then paused. Should she admit she had no idea what Henry Benson looked like? Did she want to be tossed out on her ear after coming this far? They wouldn't. Then her insecurities took over. They just might. She chewed on her bottom lip.

The young woman turned to stare at her visitor. "Is something wrong?"

"Everything is A-Okay." She hurried down the hall and found the sun room. Luck was with her. A lone gentleman sat in a rocking chair near a row of windows. His hair was white a snow, his face a road map of wrinkles. She scooted a straight-backed chair from the side of the room to sit near him. "Mr. Benson? Mr. Henry Benson?"

"Are you new here?" He squinted at her. "Where is Nancy? Is it already time to eat?"

"Not yet. I came to visit," Carole explained, "I believe you are a friend of a man I think is a relative of mine."

"I don't talk to the police no more." He accented the first syllable of police. "I done told the sheriff ever thing I know."

"I'm not a police officer." Carol moved her chair a little closer. "I believe Oliver P. Duncan was my father. Did you know him?"

Henry's cackling laugh echoed around the room. "Ollie's dead. Has been for a right smart long time."

"I know that. I am wondering if you can tell me about him. What was he like?" She held one hand with the other, and waited for Henry to reply.

After a tense spate of silence, Henry spoke again. "Don't tell me you're kin to that no-good bum."

"I think I am. I believe he was my father." Carole twisted in her chair. Her nerves were like high-tension wires. "My mother's name was Mary Elizabeth Doud Effington."

"You're Lizzie's little girl?" He scratched the side of his head. "She was a fine woman. Too bad she got mixed up with that no-good Ollie."

"Was he really no-good?"

"You wanted him to be a hero?" The old man cackled again. "Most ladies thought that about him, till they got to know him good, but he weren't."

In her mind, that was how Carole had pictured him, someone dashing, handsome, and gracious. "What was he like?"

"He was a conniving, no-good rascal. He killed his own son because he was too stingy to buy new machines. Then he let two innocent men go to jail. Blamed them, he did. One o' them men was me."

"You were a pall-bearer at his funeral," Carole said. "Why, if you have such a low opinion of him, would you do that?"

"I wanted to see him laid six-feet under and covered with dirt." The old man waved a gnarled hand in a dismissive gesture. "I don't want to talk about Ollie no more."

BILLIE HOUSTON

"One more question before I go," Carole pleaded.
"I done my time. I don't have to answer no more questions. Go on, git. Scram."
Carole quietly left the room.

Chapter Fifteen

November 19, 1974, Tuesday Afternoon

Jack took the last bowl from the dishwasher and opened a cabinet door. What a mess. Carole always kept everything in apple-pie order. The cluttered shelves that greeted him were yet another reminder of how much he depended on her to keep the house, and their lives, moving along on an even keel. He hated disarray and chaos. He needed neatness and order. He put the bowl atop an already wobbly stack and waited. It stayed. He closed the door, sat on a kitchen stool, and put his face into his hands.

He missed the peaceful home Carole maintained. He missed her on a much deeper level, too. Until she left, he never realized how much he needed her. He shook his head. He'd taken her for granted.

He had failed as a husband. He wasn't a good father, either. Carole was right about Suzanne needing discipline and structure. He had spoiled her because he loved her. Her behavior since Carole's departure showed him that was a mistake. He'd made the same mistake with Margie. He was now reaping what he'd sown.

He had, in his house, and on his hands the equivalent of two spoiled teenagers. When they weren't quarreling, they united against him and plotted ways to defy the rules he laid down.

Otis came through the back door and stopped in the kitchen entranceway. "Man, you look like death warmed over, and this house looks like a tornado hit it. What are you doing home at this time of day?"

Jack dropped his hands and lifted his head. "I came home early to straighten up a bit."

Otis sat in a kitchen chair. "Where are Suzie, 'scuse me, Suzanne and Margie?"

"Suzanne is still at school. Heaven only knows where Margie got off to."

"Good buddy, you have to take a firmer hand with those two women. They should be doing the housework around here instead of you coming home from work to clean up their messes." Otis stood. "I'll make some coffee."

"Coffee would be most welcome." So would some adult company. Jack pointed toward the coffee pot. "Wash the pot first."

Otis busied himself cleaning the pot. "You have to come down hard on those two women." He filled the pot with water and measured coffee. "If you let 'em, some women will walk all over you."

"How do you come down hard on a teenager and an emotionally retarded adult?" Jack had an aching head and a confused mind. "They are too old to turn across my knee and spank."

"There are other ways." Otis set the coffee pot on the stove and turned on the burner.

"Like what?" Jack snorted.

"Like making hard and fast rules."

"Good lord, man." Jack stood and pressed his palms across either side of his head. "Don't you think I've done that?"

"Sure you did." Otis' tone was mocking, "But you didn't stick to them. I thought Suzie was gung-ho about taking care of her daddy."

"Suzanne, please," Jack corrected automatically. "She was, at first. When Margie moved in everything changed."

"Maybe Margie is a bad influence on Suzie. Excuse me, Suzanne." Otis opened a cabinet door. A plate and three bowls fell out of the cabinet, tumbled to the floor, and splintered into pieces.

Otis raised one hand. "Stay put. I'll get this cleaned up before you can say Jack Robinson." He looked in the kitchen closet, found a broom and a dustpan, and went to work. "What does Carole think about you letting Margie live here?"

ASKING FOR A MIRACLE

"I don't think she knows." Jack hated to admit it.
"You didn't talk to her before Margie moved in?" Otis stopped sweeping and leaned on his broom. "You should have. This is her house too."
"Is it?" Jack scoffed. "She doesn't live here. She doesn't even communicate with me anymore."
"Maybe not, but Suzanne is still her daughter, and you know how Carole feels about Margie and the influence she has over Suzanne."
"Carole deserted Suzanne. She deserted me too." Jack moved to the kitchen table and sat down. "Pour the coffee."
"I don't think Carole sees it that way." Otis dumped the contents of the dustpan into the wastebasket and poured two cups of coffee.

*****

November 19, 1974
Tuesday Afternoon
Carole had spent the last two weeks researching, learning everything she could about Oliver P. Duncan. Nothing she found contradicted what Henry Benson told her. Her father was a sorry specimen of a man. All her Duncan relatives were dead. Why should that bring such sorrow? She didn't know, but it did. David was the first to go. Oliver P. Junior was killed in a hunting accident two years later. Esther passed away in nineteen thirty from cancer. Her two brothers and her sister had lived and died and she had never known them.
Oliver Duncan, Sr. lived until nineteen sixty-four. His death certificate stated his demise was from natural causes. He was eighty-two years old. Maybe the old adage about only the good dying was true. He certainly didn't die young.
From nowhere came the urge to find Jack and Suzie, to hug them and hold them close to her heart. Would they welcome her? Should she invite them to visit her? Suppose they refused. Did she dare barge into

the home she left in such haste? Did she even have the right to call that house home anymore? *Dear God, I am so confused. Please help me.*
She hadn't prayed in such a long time. Why should God heed her plea now? *Where can I turn? What can I do?* Like a clear ringing bell, the answer resonated through her mind. She found her church's telephone number, called it, and asked Evelyn, the church secretary, for an appointment to see Pastor Norman as soon as possible.
"He can see you tomorrow afternoon around three," Evelyn replied.
"I can't wait that long. This is an emergency I'll be there in thirty minutes." Carole hung up before Evelyn could reply.
Twenty-five minutes later she walked into Evelyn's office and sat down. "Forgive my rudeness, but I must see Pastor Norman."
Evelyn's sweet smile and friendly nature, usually so visible, had vanished. "He will see you. He's waiting in his office."
Carole hurried down the hall and rapped on the door marked Pastor. What was she doing here? This wasn't an emergency.
"Come in."
She opened the door and hesitated. "If you are busy, I can come back later."
Pastor Norman nodded toward the chair positioned in front of his desk. "I am never too busy to listen to a parishioner with an emergency."
Carole inched toward the chair and sat down. "I'm not sure my dilemma qualifies as an emergency. I panicked."
"Would you like something to drink? A soda, a cup of coffee?" Pastor Norman leaned back in his chair and tented his fingers. "Relax, and pull yourself together."
"Thank you for seeing me." Carol drew a deep breath.
"You left me little choice." His smile took the sting from his words. "Tell me, what's your problem?"
"My Aunt Effie passed away a few months ago."
"I know. I conducted her memorial service. It's not unusual that you are still grieving. We have a grief counselor on our staff. She holds a

session each Saturday afternoon here at the church. You don't need an appointment. The meeting starts at three o'clock."

"I don't need a grief counselor. This is something else." Was he trying to be rid of her, push her off on someone else? She was having second thoughts about coming here in the first place.

Pastor Norman bowed his head. "Pray with me, Carole."

"God wouldn't hear my prayer."

He looked up. "God always hears his children when they pray."

"I'm not sure God claims me as his child anymore." Tears flooded Carole's eyes. "I've wandered so far away. I'm not sure I can ever find my way back."

"God never changes. If you were ever His child, you are. Do you want to come back to your Heavenly Father?"

"I do, if he will have me." Carole leaned forward and gripped edge of Pastor Norman's desk. She hoped God heard her plea.

Pastor Norman reached across the desk and took her hands in his. "I will petition God on your behalf. After my prayer, you can talk to him." He bowed his head and prayed, "Father God, we come to you this afternoon with humble hearts, grateful for your many blessings. Hear our petitions, we pray. Your child Carole has wandered from you. Make her to know you are always waiting to welcome her home. Lift the heavy burden from her heart. Comfort her spirit. Bless her and her family. I ask this prayer in the name of our Lord and savior Jesus Christ. Amen."

Tears spilled from Carole's eyes and coursed down her cheeks. In that small office, holding onto the hands of a man of God, a mixture of pain and joy flooded her soul. It was a potent combination. "God, please welcome your prodigal daughter back into your fold. I..." Her voice dissolved into choking sobs. She released Pastor Norman's hands and looked up at him.

"Amen." Pastor Norman wiped a tear from his eye. "Is there something you wish to talk to me about?"

BILLIE HOUSTON

"This is in strictest confidence."
"Between you, me, and God."
Carole took a deep breath and began to speak.

Chapter Sixteen

November 24, 1974, Sunday Afternoon

Suzanne and Margie sat on the couch arguing. Their voices rose over the blare of the television.

"There are too," Suzanne asserted as she stamped one foot.

"Are not," Margie disputed. "UFOs are science fiction. I know because Mother said so."

"You and Grandma are too old to understand modern technology," Suzanne said.

Jack tried to shut out their senseless babble. To no avail. He laid his book aside. He was set to tell them both to shut up when Margie burst into tears. "Mother is old, but I'm not. You take that back."

"You are forty-seven. To me, that's ancient."

"I am not old. I will never be old. I will take my own life before I get old." Margie jumped to her feet and ran from the room.

Jack's heartburn flared. He reached for another antacid. Why hadn't he seen it before? His sister needed professional help. He was sure Suzanne's intention had not been to wound Margie so deeply. Nevertheless, she had. He could hardly ask Suzanne to apologize for something she didn't realize she'd done. This problem was larger than two teenagers arguing. He had to do something. What?

Suzanne's voice pierced his cloud of despondency.

"Aunt Margie does that every time I am about to win an argument."

He had to get Margie out of his house and someplace she could receive professional treatment. Steve would probably have some say in such a move since he was Margie's husband.

"Daddy, answer my question."

Jack jerked his thoughts back to the present. "What question?"

"I asked," Suzanne pronounced each word slowly and distinctly, "Do you think I hurt Aunt Margie's feelings?" She tagged her question with a meek, "I didn't mean to."

"Maybe you should tell her that." Jack's body broke into a cold sweat. "Find her and make your peace. I am going to visit your mother."

"I'm going to Cindy's." Suzanne headed for the stairs. "I'll apologize to Aunt Margie and then tell her we're going out, so she won't come down later, find us gone, and worry."

His own child was a complete enigma to him. One minute she wounded her aunt without knowing. The next minute she showed concern for her welfare. "Be home before eight." Jack debated with himself if he should telephone Carole before calling on her. He hadn't seen her in over two months. That was a long time. "Too long." *Think too long is never act.* "I'm going." He found a windbreaker in the foyer closet and grabbed his car keys.

*****

November 24, 1974
Sunday Afternoon
Nothing around her had changed, but Carole had. Since last Tuesday when she talked and prayed with Pastor Norman, she was different inside. How could she have wandered so far away from a savior who loved her? She laid her Bible on the couch cushion beside her, and closed her eyes. The last verse she read played over and over through her head. Like some half-forgotten old hymn, it soothed her troubled soul. *And be ye kind one to another, tenderhearted, forgiving one another, even as God, for Christ's sake, hath forgiven you.* Ephesians 4:32 KJV.

Small wonder Jack never accepted Christ as his savior. The only Bible he read was his wife's life. What a terrible example she had been. *God forgive me.* "I can't change the past, but I can tell Jack I'm sorry for my past behavior." If God could forgive her and take her back into his fold, surely she could forgive Jack for something that happened over twenty years ago.

She had gone off chasing some foolish dream of a heroic father who loved her. The bitter truth was her father had been a selfish, unfeeling man who used the people around him for his own purposes. She had to find some way to forgive him, not only for his neglect of her, but for destroying her mother's life.

My mother. How much she gave up for her baby. She lost the joy of claiming her child to protect that child from being an outcast. Sorrow, like a heavy wedge, lodged in Carole's stomach.

A knock on the front door pulled her from her dark musings. She slipped her feet into her shoes and hurried to yank it open.

Jack stood on the other side. He hunched his shoulders. His hands were shoved in the pocket of his windbreaker. A chilly north wind ruffled his hair.

He announced, without preamble, "I need to talk to you."

She swung the door wider. "Come in." Happiness sang through her body. He had come to her, at last. That had to be good news.

He entered with some reluctance. Cold wind from outside entered with him. "I should have called first."

His tone and stance put distance between them. Was he angry? Hurt? Repulsed? In a few short months he had become a stranger. In so short a time, how far apart they had drifted. She extended one hand. "Would you like to sit down?" Her voice rang hollow in her own ears.

He sat on one end of the couch. "I am sorry to intrude."

"You're not intruding. I'm glad you are here. I have so many things to tell you." She had missed their friendly conversations. "I visited with Pastor Norman last Tuesday—"

"That's good, but can we talk about religion another time? Right now, we have more pressing problems to deal with."

She had made a decision of great magnitude and he dismissed it as a trivial event. Her disappointment ran deep. Her hurt ran deeper.

BILLIE HOUSTON

Belatedly, his last statement registered in her brain. "Pressing problems? Like what?"

Chapter Seventeen

November 24, 1974, Sunday Afternoon

Jack was caught in a double bind. If he told Carol how bad things were at home, she would be displeased, even angry. At the same time, he owed her the truth. Maybe she already knew about Margie. Perhaps Midge, who made it her business to stay abreast of all the latest gossip, had told her. "Have you talked to Midge lately?"

Carole actually smiled. "I know you don't like Midge. You never have. I hope you don't expect me to stop seeing my best friend."

"No, not at all." So much for that approach. "You and I have been out of touch for some time."

"So much as happened to me in that short time." Carole looked down at the floor. "I don't know where to start."

It's now or never. "We can start with me telling you what I came here to say. I love you. I need you. My life is a mess without you. Will you come home? You can dictate the terms." He paused briefly before going on. He spoke swiftly, hurrying to utter words he hated saying. "Margie is living with Suzanne and me. She and Steve separated again. She's afraid to live alone. Mother won't take her in."

Carole looked up and opened her mouth to speak.

Jack held up one hand. "No, please. Let me finish. I suspect Margie may be suicidal. She needs professional help. I will get that help for her, if Steve will agree." *There, I've said it.*

Carole's eyes held a look of compassionate understanding. "I have felt for a long time Margie had problems, but suicide? I never thought it was that bad." She reached across the space that separated them and took his hand in hers. "I deserted you when you needed me. I'm sorry."

Jack had waited so long for this moment. "Can we start over? I'll be a better husband this time."

"Jack." Her voice was velvet-soft. "I love you, too." She slid across the couch and put her arms around his neck. "Kiss me, and tell me again that you love me."

He drew her closer and kissed her with passion before looking into her eyes. "I do love you, Carole, with every beat of my heart." A flame of desire burst inside him. It blazed into a hunger such as he had never known before. *This is the way it should have been all along.* He broke the embrace. "You felt it too, didn't you?"

Carole ran shaking fingers over her lips. "I did, and it was wonderful." Lingering fears moved in to chase away Jack's burst of desire. "Will you come home? I know how you feel about Margie—"

"Did you mean it when you said I could dictate the terms?"

Jack's answer was a resounding, "Yes."

"I have to share a recent experience with you." Carole moved back to her former place at the end of the couch.

What has she done? Had she already found someone else? "I'm listening."

"It's about last Tuesday when I called on Pastor Norman."

Did she go there to confess some sin? Has she been unfaithful to him? His bones turned to water. He was going to be physically ill.

"I rededicated my life to Jesus." Her smile was radiant. Her face glowed. "Isn't that wonderful? I haven't known peace such as this since I was a teenager and first came to know Him as my savior."

Jack didn't know if he should laugh or cry. He was too stunned to speak. He was both relieved and angry. Relieved she hadn't broken her marriage vows. Angry she was making such a major event from so trivial a happening. He finally found his voice. "That's nice."

"I will help you with Margie. We will find a place for her. My only stipulation to coming home is that you and Suzanne, and Margie—so

ASKING FOR A MIRACLE

long as she is there—attend church services with me Sunday morning, Sunday evening, and Wednesday evening."

"You know how I feel about religion." Surprise caught in Jack's throat and hung there.

"Please, just give church-going a chance. That's all I ask. After hearing Pastor Norman preach a few sermons, I believe you will change your mind." She turned that dazzling smile in his direction. "All you need to do is hear the gospel preached. The Holy spirit will do the rest."

"Stop all this babble about spirits and sermons." How could an otherwise sensible woman hold to such primitive beliefs? He was reluctant to admit, even to himself that he was afraid to venture into the realm of religion. He would fail miserably in an attempt to live a perfect life. "Please, Carole, come home. I need you. Suzanne needs you."

The radiance drained from her face. "You said you would do what I asked if I would come home. Please, can't we just try my way?"

"I can't live with trying to unravel all that religious mumbo-jumbo."

"It's not a religion, and it's not mumbo-jumbo." Tears rolled down her cheeks. "You promised, Jack. You promised."

He stood, feeling small and sick, and betrayed. "I'm through begging. I'll go now. If and when you come home it will be because you ask me to let you." He walked out the door, leaving a weeping woman calling after him.

Chapter Eighteen

November 25, 1974, Monday Morning
Carole woke with a start, completely disoriented. After a few seconds, she realized she'd fallen asleep on the couch. Her neck was stiff, her eyes were puffy from crying, and she had a splitting headache. Aunt Effie's grandfather clock chimed three o'clock in the morning.

Events from the night before crowded in around her pain. It was followed by a tidal wave of desolation. She prayed so hard, believed so completely. She closed her eyes against the throbbing pain that beat behind them. Was God's answer to her prayers no? There was a time in her life when she would have been angered by such a possibility. Heartbreak and experience had taught her two hard lessons. One was, God doesn't make mistakes. Another was, He led his children through trials and tribulations, not to punish them, but to teach them. She bowed her head. "Heavenly Father, what are you trying to teach me? Show me, and help me to learn and accept it. Not my will, but thine be done."

The ringing of her telephone brought her head up. A phone call at this hour of the morning was bound to bring bad news. She lifted the receiver to her ear. "Hello."

"Mom, this is Suzie. Something terrible has happened. Daddy's been in an automobile accident. He's at Mercy Hospital."

"Is he badly hurt?" Grizzly, roadside scenes paraded through Carole's mind, sights of bloody, mangled bodies and twisted, smashed vehicles. Her world tilted and spun. She blinked her eyes and struggled to hold on to consciousness "Are you at the hospital now?"

"Yes, oh, come Mom, quickly. We need you. Daddy is in the emergency room and Margie is freaking out."

"I'll be there soon. Hang on sweetie." Carole hung up the phone, dressed, slipped her feet into her shoes, grabbed a jacket, and her handbag, and ran for the door.

She arrived at the almost-deserted emergency waiting room to find Suzie huddled in a corner, fear written on her young face and tears streaming from her eyes, Margie crying and walking the floor, and Clarissa sitting in an ancient straight-back chair, complaining about not being allowed to see her son.

The moment Carole entered the room, Suzie ran to meet her and threw both arms around her neck. "Mom, I'm so glad you're here." Wrenching sobs tore from her throat.

"What happened?" She held her daughter in a close embrace.

"Daddy is in the emergency room. A car going the wrong way on Highway 281 hit him head–on."

"How badly is he hurt?" Carole's knees turned to water. She released her daughter and sank into a chair. *Dear God, please don't let him die.*

A dry-eyed Clarissa intruded into the conversation. "They won't tell us anything."

"They don't know anything yet, Grandma." Suzie wiped at a tear.

"They do know," Margie cried, hysteria unraveling in her voice. "It's so bad they don't want to tell us." She cried even louder. "What if he's dead?"

"This kind of behavior will get us nowhere." *Please dear Savior, help me to hold on.* "Margie, I'm surprised someone hasn't thrown you out of here before now. Quiet down, and sit." To her great surprise her sister-in-law obeyed, and sat in the chair next to her.

Steve came through the door, looking pale and disheveled. "I came as soon as I heard. How bad is he?"

Margie half stood. "Oh, Steve—"

Carole grabbed her shirttail and pulled her back into her chair. "We don't know yet." She held onto Margie's shirttail. "Thank you for

coming." The clock on the wall read four-fifteen. "How did you find out?"
"One of my employees called me. His wife is a nurse here at the hospital." He sat on the other side of Margie, and took her hand. "You're being very brave about this. I expected to find you in hysterics." He took her hand in his. "I'm proud of you."
Clarissa made a sound deep in her throat. "Well, I must say—"
"Clarissa," Carole spoke before she thought. "This is neither the time nor the place."
A gray-haired man wearing a white coat came down the hallway and stopped just inside the emergency room entranceway. He looked around the room before asking, "Is one of you Mrs. Jackson Garner?"
"I'm Mrs. Garner." Carol stood on wobbly legs.
Simultaneously, Clarissa rose and pushed back her chair. "I, too, am Mrs. Garner."
"I'm Doctor Williams." The man ran a hand across his brow. "I should have been more specific. I am looking for Jackson Garner's wife." He nodded in Carole's direction. "I assume that is you."
She nodded. "Yes."
"Come with me." Doctor Williams motioned with one hand as he headed down the hall.
Carole followed the doctor.
Clarissa followed along behind her daughter-in-law. "I'm coming too. Jack is my son, my only son."
Doctor Williams slid to a halt. "Sorry, but not this time. My business is with—" He looked at Carole with a raised eyebrow.
"Carole."
"My business is with Carole."
Clarissa was not that easily deterred. "Anything that concerns my son concerns me."
"Will you go back to the emergency room or shall I call security?" He raked the older woman's face with a scathing stare.

"You superiors will hear of this," Clarissa promised, as she turned in the direction of the waiting room.

Carole hurried to keep pace with Doctor Williams. He led the way to a small office, opened the door, and sat behind a tiny desk. He gestured toward a nearby chair.

Carole sat and grasped the arms of the chair. She shook with shock and fright. "What happened? Is Jack going to be all right?"

"Your husband was involved in a head-on collision. He must have seen the car approaching from the wrong way. He tried to get out of the way by pulling off the road. He didn't make it. He was braced for the hit. The severest injuries are to his lower extremities. He also has some broken ribs, a broken arm, cuts and lacerations and a concussion. Since we haven't completed our internal examination, I can't say about further injuries."

"Will he be all right?" Panic rose in Carole's throat and hung there. "Will he walk again?"

"I wish I could answer both questions in the affirmative." Doctor Williams clasped his hands together and placed them on the desk in front of him. "Your husband lost his left leg. It was crushed by the impact of the smash-up. We removed the mangled limb just below the knee. If he makes it through the night, we can talk later about the injuries to his other knee and ankle."

"If?" This was a bad dream, a nightmare of the worst kind. "Are you telling me he might die?"

"We will do everything we can." Doctor Williams stood. "I must get back to my patient."

"May I see Jack?"

"Maybe tomorrow. Go home and get some rest." He opened the door. "We will know more tomorrow."

Carole headed in the direction of the waiting room. Jack had lost his left leg. He could die this very night. The thought terrified her. *Please, God, don't let that happen. Don't take him from me now.*

Chapter Nineteen

January 14, 1975, Tuesday Morning

The hum of voices broke through Jack's shell of pain. Where was he? How did he get here? Remembrance came slowly. The car approaching, the fear that grabbed him, the impact, the pain, and then blessed oblivion. He opened his eyes, and saw only blurs. Was he blind?

"How is he this morning?"

"Carole." That voice he would know anywhere. The mist slowly cleared. Carole and a white-coated man came toward him. One of his legs was in traction, the other extended no further than just below his knee. The stump end was swathed in bandages. He closed his eyes. He wasn't dead, but wished he were.

"He opened his eyes and spoke my name," Carole said.

The middle-aged man shook his head. "You were imagining things. He's in a coma."

"I swear. Doctor Williams, he opened his eyes and said 'Carole.'"

Jack opened his eyes again.

"By Jove..." Doctor Williams lifted Jack's wrist and felt his pulse. "It's a miracle."

"Thank God." Carole choked on a sob.

How long have I been in this place? He was slipping again, back into the darkness of that nether world he came from. Carole's voice called to him, "No, Jack, no. Don't leave me."

He opened his eyes. "How long have I been here?"

"Three weeks and two days." Carole smiled through her tears. "Welcome back, darling. If you will let me, I'll come home and care for you."

Words he said to her the night of his accident ran through his head to curse and taunt him. If and when she came home it would be because she asked him to let her. Was she asking now because she pitied him? He wanted her, but not under the existing circumstances. He was not the man he once was, and he never would be again. If he could have turned from her, he would have. There must be some veteran's hospital he could retreat to. "That's kind of you, but it's not necessary."

*****

February 14, 1975
Friday Morning
Someone shaking his shoulder stirred Jack to wakefulness. Nurse Brown wore a crisp white uniform and stood beside his bedside. "Good morning, Mr. Garner. It's time for breakfast." She pulled the rolling tray she had in tow across his bed, and set the brake. "Can you manage alone, or shall I help you?"
"I can manage, thank you." The bitterness that ran through Jack's veins seeped out into his voice. He lifted the lid on a bowl. "Oatmeal." He replaced the lid. "I am sick and tired of oatmeal for breakfast."
"Now that your leg is healing, and your arm out of a cast, you will be going home soon." She poured cream in his coffee, and put sugar and milk on his oatmeal. "Maybe your wife will make you an omelet." She retrieved a chair from across the room and sat down.
There should be a law against anyone being so cheerful this early in the morning. "I am not going home. I'm going to a veteran's hospital."
Nurse Brown gave him the spoon. "Eat your breakfast and you will feel better."
Suzanne stopped in the doorway and knocked on the wall before entering. "Hi Daddy. How are you feeling this morning?"
"Worse, thank you," Jack replied. What a question to ask a man who, over the last four months, had endured multiple surgeries and constant pain.

"I'll do that, Ruth." Suzanne came to stand beside the nurse.

Nurse Brown stood and extended one hand. "Sit here. See if you can persuade your father to eat something. Will you be here a while?"

"Yes. Mom will be here later." Suzanne sat. "We are taking Daddy home today."

"I'll come by later and help you check out." Nurse Brown headed for the door.

Don't hurry," Suzanne called after her. She focused her attention on her father. "Are you going to eat your breakfast?"

"You seem to know Nurse Brown quite well. How long have you two been friends?"

"Daddy," Suzanne spoke with all the indignation of youth. "You have been in this hospital for four months. I am on first-name basis with most of the nurses and half the supporting staff."

Jack could think of no answer to that.

After an uncomfortable span of silence, Suzanne spoke again, "Don't be so glum. This is Valentine's Day, a time to be in love and happy."

He would always be in love with Carol. Why didn't he know sooner? He doubted he would ever be happy again. Jack stared into space. He was a middle-aged, disabled, shell of a man who had made a total mess of his life.

"Daddy," Suzanne's voice impinged on his dismal thoughts.

"What?"

"You're not listening to me. That's what."

"I'm sorry. What did you say?"

"I said," Suzanne pronounced each word distinctly, "Mom is talking to Doctor Williams. She will be here soon and we can take you home and be a family again, just like before.

Jack knew nothing was ever going to be 'just like before' again.

*****

Doctor Williams leaned back in his chair and stared across his desk toward Carole. "I wish you would consider leaving Jack in the hospital for another month or so. He's still recovering. Our rehabilitation center is well equipped to help him adjust to the challenge of learning to live with a prosthesis. It's not an easy transition, and..."

"I can't afford to pay the hospital to do something I can do myself." Jack's hospital and doctor bills had dipped heavily into their savings. "I promise to keep up the program of activities he has begun here."

"Maybe his attitude will improve once he's home." Doctor Williams shook his head. "He needs to eat a healthy diet to have the strength to work hard. He refuses to eat and complains constantly about the food here. He must begin to carry out daily activities. Here he refuses to get out of bed. You will need the help of a therapist to teach him to use his prosthesis. I will prescribe something to help him control his pain. Be sure you—"

Carole waved one hand. "I know what to do, Doctor. Rest assured I will see after Jack with tender loving care."

Doctor Williams pushed back his chair. "Don't wear yourself down. If it gets to be more than you can handle, call for help."

Chapter Twenty

April 16, 1975, Wednesday Morning

Carole sat on the couch and rubbed her forehead with her fingertips. Ten o'clock in the morning and she was already tired. The past few months had been a nightmare. The coming months showed no signs of being any different. From the moment Jack was carried into the house and put on the bed in the den-turned-bedroom, he had done nothing but rebel and complain. He first objected to being put in the den. "I don't like it here. Why can't I be in my own bedroom upstairs where I can have some privacy?"

Carole tried to explain how difficult it would be for her to climb those stairs a dozen times a day to care for him.

Her pleas for his understanding went unheeded.

"What about *my* comfort? There is no en suite bathroom down here."

"You should be up and moving around. A walk down the hall a few times a day will do you good." She bit her lip to keep from saying more. In the beginning Carole schooled herself to ignore his snide remarks and his constant nitpicking. After two weeks of his unconscionable behavior, she snapped back with a barbed reply of her own. She was immediately sorry. "I didn't mean to be cross."

"Yes, you did. When are you going to relent and let me go to a veterans' hospital?"

It was not his words, but his tone of voice that reignited her temper. "If you went that far away, we couldn't afford to visit you. We barely have enough to pay our bills and exist from week to week."

Over the next weeks Jack moved from carping to sullen, speaking only when he was spoken to.

BILLIE HOUSTON

This can't go on, Carole told herself. *I have to do something if I want to keep my sanity.*

After Jack's accident, Carole prayed long and earnestly for a miracle, for God to let her husband live. She vowed to nurse him back to health, and dedicate the remainder of her life caring for him. She'd received her miracle. She also got more problems than she bargained for. Not the least of those problems was financial. Jack's hospital and doctor bills were draining their savings. She struggled to buy food and pay bills with Jack's income from the hardware store. When she learned how those profits were shared, Carole exploded. Clarissa received the lions share. When she broached the subject to Jack, he shrugged. "That's the way Dad set things up."

Carole made no reply. She didn't want to upset her ailing husband.

Her largest worry crowded in around other depressing thoughts. Suzanne's graduation was less than three months away. How would she manage to pay for a ring, graduation announcements, a cap and gown, a formal for her daughter's senior prom, and any other unforeseen expenses? She wanted this to be such a happy time for Suzanne. Carole lifted her chin. If she could make it so, it will be.

Even as she picked up the telephone, she knew what she was about to do was wrong. How easy it was to justify her actions. She had to look out for her daughter. If that meant stooping to deceitfulness, she would. She called Steve, who had stepped into Jack's shoes, and was running the store. He would always have her eternal gratitude. He also moved Margie back into their house, and agreed to live there with her. Carole wondered how far "living with her" went. She didn't dare ask. Why look a gift horse in the mouth?

Steve's voice called her back from her gloomy thoughts. "Carole, is something wrong? Has Jack taken a turn for the worse?"

"Everything is wrong, and Jack is his usual disagreeable self."

"You are in a blue funk." Steve let go with a mirthless chuckle before his voice took on a serious tone. "I hate to trouble you with more bad news, but Clarissa was in to see me today. She has decided to take over running the store until Jack can come back to work."

"She can't do that. Clarissa knows nothing about running a hardware store. She will ruin Jack's business." That would be the last straw for Jack. It would destroy him. Carole spoke with quiet but desperate determination. "I have to stop her."

"I don't think you can stop her," Steve replied.

"I think I can." Carole's mind raced at a feverish pitch. *It's worth a try.* "How long before you can be over here with Jack's lawyer, a durable power of attorney, two witnesses, and a notary?"

Steve sputtered before saying. "Is one o'clock okay?" He tagged his question with another query. "What are you up to?"

"I'm up to my neck in bills and sick and tired of Clarissa living like an heiress while my daughter does without things she wants and needs."

"The hardware store belongs to Jack," Steve reminded her, not unkindly. "In case of his death it passes on to Clarissa and Margie. Clarissa says Jack's illness is reason enough for her to step in and take over. The division of profits is a part of Edgar's will. If you try to change that, Clarissa will fight you all the way to the Supreme Court."

"I'm not planning to tamper with Edgar Garner's will. I do plan to set about making some changes." Carole ignored the still small voice in the back of her head that whispered, over and over, *you are expecting God's help to pull off something so underhanded. Really, Carole?* She pushed that admonition to the back of her mind.

"If you need Margie's monthly allowance," Steve said, "I'm sure she wouldn't object."

"Margie's allowance is a mere pittance compared to what Clarissa knocks down each month." Carole was so engrossed in her own problems she had forgotten to ask. "How is Margie?"

"Margie is doing better. She's seeing a psychiatrist once a week. He prescribed a mood stabilizer." A note of pride sounded in Steve's reply. "She's working here at the store, in the garden center, and she loves it."

"That's wonderful, I—"
"I have to run. I'm needed on the docks. See you around one."
Carole hung up the phone. She wondered if God would forgive her for what might be a little devious. That nagging little voice surfaced once more. Yes. She knew what she was doing was morally dishonest. Once again, she ignored it. She had to do what she had to do.

*****

Jack's depression deepened with each passing day. His life no longer had any purpose or meaning. He was of no earthly use to anyone, and a burden to Carole. She never complained, but he knew he provoked her to anger many times. That was his intent. If he made her life unbearable, she would put him away somewhere and be free of him once and for all. He seriously considered suicide. Had he been able to get up and move about, he would have taken an overdose of his sleeping pills, or found a sharp razor blade.
Carole came in with his food tray. "Lunch time." She set his tray before him.
"I'm not hungry." He turned to face away from her.
"Steve will be here soon with your attorney, and two witnesses." She pulled a chair near his bed and sat down. "I'm asking you to grant me your power of attorney. I want to be able to act in your stead and run the store until you are well again."
"Steve can do that quite well."
"Your mother doesn't think so. She has told him to go back to being manager of the automotive department. She's set to take his place."
Jack turned to face her. "Why would you want to take on my mother in a battle you are sure to lose?"
"I love you, Jack," Carole answered. "I didn't know how much until I thought I was going to lose you." Unshed tears moistened her eyes. "I need your signature. Steve will still run the store. I'm going to work in the appliance department."

ASKING FOR A MIRACLE

"What happens to me?" He had thought he was immune to any kind of emotion. He was wrong. The thought of going to some hospital far away brought a sharp sting of pain.

"You get well as swiftly as possible. I'm hiring a male nurse to care for you during the day. I'm also hiring a housekeeper. My wages will pay for their services."

Jack exploded. "No." He appended his declaration with a questioning, "Why?"

"It's simple." Carole spread her hands. "Clarissa will destroy your business if she takes control. If you love me and trust me, you will do this for me. The ball is in your court."

Chapter Twenty-One

May 21, 1975, Tuesday Evening

Carole sat in the glider on her patio and watched a waning gibbous moon shine like a jewel in the night sky. So far, her plan was working well. Ralph Warren, the man she hired to be Jack's nurse, was a Godsend, as he should be since she met him at church. When she was first introduced to him, a tall, muscular military retiree, his polite demeanor that was coupled with a no-nonsense attitude impressed her. Later she learned he was a nurse and looking for a job. They talked, and she hired him.

Although Jack would never admit it, she knew he liked Ralph.

"The man is a tyrant," Jack had told her. "Do you know what he said to me today? He said, 'Stop feeling sorry for yourself and get on with your therapy, and your life.'" Remembering made Carole smile. Despite Jack's refusal to cooperate, and his constant complaining, Ralph plodded steadily along with his treatment plan.

With the salary she made working, Carole could pay Ralph and Mrs. Dennis, the housekeeper she had hired. She could, with careful budgeting, also ensure that Suzanne's graduation went well. Carole's salary, and the raise she gave Steve and Jack, cut deeply into her mother-in-law's monthly income. How long would it be before Clarissa showed up with fire in her eyes and venom on her tongue?

Clarissa showed up at the hardware store three mornings in a row. The amount of hard work required to run a successful hardware business, coupled with the fact that she must spend an hour or so each day on the dock, soon dampened her enthusiasm. She left the third evening with the promise to Steve that she would drop in soon to see how things were going. Soon had yet to come.

BILLIE HOUSTON

Two months passed and in a matter of days, Clarissa's monthly check was due again. Could it be, that by some miracle, she was not going to complain?

"Mom?" Suzanne opened the sliding door and came outside. "Could you use some company?"

"If that company is you, yes." Carole patted the space next to her. "We haven't had a heart-to-heart talk in a long time."

Suzanne came to sit beside her mother. "Why are you sitting out here all alone?" Before Carole could answer, she said, "I think I have a problem."

"You think?" Carole raised an eyebrow.

"I know I do."

"Do you want to talk about it?"

"Yes." Suzanne sighed. "Look at that moon. Isn't it beautiful?"

"Yes, it is," Carole answered, and then sat waiting for Suzanne to speak. Several minutes ticked by before she said, "Two boys have invited me to the prom next Friday. Rick Welch asked me last Sunday after church. Luke Maddox asked me today after study hall."

"Did you accept Rick's invitation?" Carole liked Rick Welch. He was a nice young man from a good Christian family. She wasn't acquainted with Luke Maddox personally. She did know him by reputation. She didn't want Suzanne anywhere near that boy.

"Sort of." Suzanne frowned.

"You can't 'sort of' accept an invitation. Either you did or you didn't."

"I did." Suzanne huffed out an aggravated sigh. "But Luke is so popular, and every girl in school wants to date him."

Carole wanted to tell her daughter she couldn't go anywhere with Luke Maddox. That would be the worst thing she could do. "I can't answer that question for you. You have to decide for yourself. Have you prayed about this?"

"Do you think God would listen?"

"I don't know why He wouldn't," Carole replied.

ASKING FOR A MIRACLE

"Because it's a silly question. God doesn't have time to listen to me asking him about which boy to date for my prom."
"God always has time to hear his children's prayers." Carole put her arm around her daughter's shoulders. "Would you like me to pray with you?"
Suzanne nodded.
Carole took her daughter's hand and they bowed their heads. "'Heavenly Father, Suzanne and I come to you tonight with humble hearts asking you to forgive us of our sins and hear our prayer. Suzanne has accepted Rick's invitation to go to the prom with him. Luke asked her later. Show her what you would have her do. Bless us and bless Daddy. Help him to get well soon. I ask this prayer in the name of my blessed savior, Jesus Christ. Amen."
Suzanne raised her head. She squeezed her mother's hand. "Mom, you have power. I felt it flowing from you when you prayed."
"What you felt was the power of the Holy Spirit." Carole returned her squeeze. "That same Spirit lives in you, if you believe Jesus died for your sins, and accept Him as your savior."
"I have believed that since I was fourteen years old." Suzanne wiped at a stray tear. "Don't you remember the Sunday I joined the church?"
"People join churches every day. That doesn't mean they have trusted Christ as their savior." What a sorry parent she had been. She prayed for God's forgiveness and His help her teach her child His ways.
"I did believe, Mom. I believed with all my heart. I still do."
"Do you think you can make a decision now?"
"I already have." Suzanne looked up at the moon and smiled. "The moment you said, 'Show her what you would have her do', I saw how wrong it would be to break my date with Rick. He's not popular or macho like Luke is, but I think Jesus likes him better than He likes Luke. Maybe I do too." She kissed her mother's cheek. "I'm going to bed. I can sleep now."
She was glad somebody could. "Goodnight, sweetie."

BILLIE HOUSTON

Carole sat alone, staring at the moon and wondering how she could have been so recently careless about her Christian walk. "I should have prayed about my rash decision to undermine Clarissa, and then waited on Him for His answer. She said, to no one in particular, "I shouldn't have done it, but it seemed the only way. Was I wrong?"
"Talking to yourself?"
She turned to see Ralph standing in the doorway. She jumped to her feet. "I should have been in to relieve you thirty minutes ago, I'm sorry."
"I forgive you, and may I make a suggestion? When in doubt, try talking to God." He slid the door back.
Carole preceded him inside. *Now he tells me.*

Chapter Twenty-Two

June 2, 1975, Monday Morning

Jack laid his newspaper on his breakfast tray as Ralph entered the room with a towel slung over his shoulder and carrying a basin of warm water. "Ready for your bath?"

"I am, indeed." In spite of his early struggle to dislike this man, Jack had grown very fond of Ralph Warren. "Did you know that West Point has begun accepting women? What do you, as a military man, think of that?"

"I have no objections." Ralph set the basin on the table beside Jack's bed.

"Do you? You were in the military."

There was a time when Jack would have said he did. The past seven months had changed his point of view on so many things. "I—don't know. A lot of ideas have shifted in my head since my accident. Do you think women will make good leaders?"

"Women have been in the military for some time now. They make excellent soldiers. I met my wife in the service." A smile spread across Ralph's face. "At the time she outranked me. Sit up and take off your pajama top. After your bath, we will put a compression garment on your stump and try standing on your temporary prosthesis."

"I'm not going to go through trying to do the impossible. My stump is still swollen." Jack grabbed the opening of his pajama top. "It's time I accepted I am never going to walk and admit to what is."

Ralph stood waiting for Jack to move his hands. "Your stump will eventually get to its normal size. Meanwhile a compression garment will help reduce your swelling and help prevent fluid build-up inside and around your stump. If you continue to refuse to work toward rehabilitation, eventually some of your muscles will atrophy."

"I said." Jack tightened his grip. "I'm not putting myself through this useless torture, and I'm not."

"Spoken like a true quitter." Ralph pulled Jack's hands from the front of his pajama top and began the process of loosening the buttons on his pajama top.

"You have no right to say that to me." Jack raised his voice. "You don't have any idea how much pain I have endured. Or how much I hate being tied to this bed, having someone care for me as if I were a baby."

"I would feel sorry for you if you didn't feel so sorry for yourself." Ralph completed bathing Jack and helped him into clean pajamas. I'll be back soon to see if you changed your mind."

Jack was still fuming fifteen minutes later when Otis came through the door. "Hi buddy, how's it going this morning?"

"'It's not going, but Ralph is. If Carole doesn't fire that man, I will."

"What are you in a snit about now?" Otis sat in the chair beside Jack's bed.

"The man insulted me. He called me a quitter."

"How's using the temporary prosthesis going?"

"It isn't, not that it's any of your business." Jack put his hand to his forehead and sighed. "I am never going to walk again. I have accepted that."

"I should have left you in that fox hole instead of dragging you all the way back to a MASH unit. You could have died there and been saved all this misery. Better still, you could have landed in a prisoner-of-war-camp and really found out about suffering."

Jack was appalled that his long-time best friend would speak to him with such disrespect. "If I could, I would get out of this bed and beat you to a pulp."

Otis stood. "But you can't. So long, buddy. I'll be back when you cool down a little." He turned, and without looking back, walked from the room.

ASKING FOR A MIRACLE

Jack lay there, in that miserable bed, turning over thoughts in his mind, trying to clear away some of the confusion that plagued him, until he dropped into a dreamless sleep.
Ralph coming into the room awakened him. "Where have you been?"
"I've been doing a little praying and a little repenting." Ralph sat in the chair by Jack's bed. "I owe you an apology for what I said to you earlier this morning. I take my nursing duties very seriously. I should have been encouraging you, not making unkind remarks. I'm sorry."
Ralph was the embodiment of manliness. That he would admit to making mistakes and praying for forgiveness, amazed Jack. "You actually prayed to God?"
"I got down on my knees, bowed my head and asked for forgiveness. Does that surprise you?"
It did, and Jack said so before asking, "Why?"
"I felt I had violated a sacred trust. I needed forgiveness."
"Are you telling me that you accept as true all that mumbo-jumbo about people rising from the dead, and spirits, and angels?" Jack couldn't believe what he was hearing.
"I am telling you I believe that Jesus Christ is the only son of almighty God. I believe he died on the cross for our sins, and offers salvation and eternal life to all who trust and accept him." A puzzled frown pleated Ralph's brow. "Are you telling me you don't?"
Jack shrugged. "Not really. I don't put much stock in the supernatural."
"Can I ask you a personal question?" Ralph rubbed his thumb and forefinger along his chin. "I want an honest answer."
"Shoot." Jack had been in religious arguments many times before. If some kind of trick question was coming, he was well prepared for it.
"When you saw that car coming toward you the wrong way down a one-way highway, what were your thoughts?"
Jack's mind harked back to that night of terror. "I was hoping and praying I could get out of the way before I got killed, or killed somebody else, or both."

"You were praying?" Ralph leaned forward and narrowed his eyes. "To whom?"

"I don't know." Discomfort crowded in around Jack's assurance. "Whatever God that exists, I suppose."

"So, you do admit there is a God?"

Jack conceded, but reluctantly. "I agree there is some higher being that exists somewhere in the universe. It's all that talk about spirits and some man rising from the dead that I can't accept."

Ralph stood. "I'll bring your lunch." He turned to go.

Jack called after him. "Wait a minute."

Ralph stopped and turned. "Yes?"

"That's the end of our conversation? You're not going to tell me how wrong I am?"

"Would it do any good?" Ralph retraced his footsteps and sat in the chair he had recently vacated. "Do you love golf?"

That seemed a strange question, nevertheless, Jack answered, "I wouldn't call it love. I do like to play and to watch. It's my favorite sport."

"How about Carole? Do you love her?"

This man was trying to get under his skin. Jack was not about to let him see how well he was succeeding. "Of course, I love her. She's my wife. What does that have to do with religion?"

"Nothing at all, but it has everything to do with Christianity, whose foundation is anchored in divine love."

"If you are trying to confuse me, you are doing a fine job." Jack jabbed his pillow with his fist. "Tell me straight what you are trying to say."

"I'm saying that accepting Christ and believing is a heart-felt matter. It's comparable to your love for Carole. Divine love is a matter of faith and trust. The Holy Spirit must speak to you for you to experience salvation. It's not a game like golf. It's a lifetime commitment." Once again, he stood. "I'll bring your lunch." He walked from the room leaving a confused man staring after him.

Chapter Twenty-Three

June 7, 1975, Saturday Morning

Carole turned from dusting shelves to seeing Clarissa barreling down the aisle of the hardware store with her arms rigid at her sides, and both hands clenched into fists. *The day of reckoning has come.* She stiffened her backbone, laid her duster aside and waited for what promised to be a nasty confrontation.

Clarissa stopped before the small appliances shelf, pointed a forefinger in Carole's direction, and shouted, "Thief. That's what you are, a low-down, conniving, common thief."

The few customers nearby turned to stare at them.

Carole stepped from behind the counter and stood face-to-face with her mother-in-law. She had on the tip of her tongue to tell this woman what a poor excuse for a human being she was. Words from Proverbs 15:1 ran through her mind. *A soft answer turneth away wrath, but grievous words stir up anger.*

"Good morning, Clarissa." It would be difficult for her to judge which person was more surprised by her response, Carole or her mother-in-law.

Clarissa blinked and swallowed. "This is not a good morning. I have some things to say to you before I consider taking legal action against you."

"Not here," Carole looked around at the few staring customers. "This way. We can go to Jack's office."

"I happen to know Steve now occupies that office." Clarissa fell in step with Carole, mumbling threats and dire promises under her breath, as they made their way to the back of the store that housed the office area.

Carole was opening the office door when Clarissa stopped short. "What malicious conspiracy are you plotting? Is Steve your accomplice?"

"I am standing in for Jack until he's well enough to return." Carole entered the office. "Steve is my assistant."

"When will Jack be able to return?" Clarissa followed her inside.

"Maybe in a few months, maybe never." To her utter surprise, Clarissa burst into tears. "Is Jack dying?"

"No, no." Was it pity she felt for this selfish, overbearing woman? She sat behind Jack's worn old desk, and pointed to a chair. "Jack has given up hope of ever walking again."

Clarissa dropped into the chair and bowed her head. "It's not like Jack to give up. Does he know you are stealing money from his company?" She answered her own question. "Of course, he doesn't." She added a barbed accusation that went through Carole like an arrow. "And you call yourself a Christian."

It struck her heart with cruel accuracy. Her underhanded actions have impaired her Christian testimony. From the beginning she had known what she was doing was questionable. What she must do now came to her like an epiphany. She must confess, make this right, and trust God to care for her and her family. Clarissa had won, but so had she. Being right with God was far more important than winning her battle with her mother-in-law.

"You certainly don't act like a Christian. Really, Carole."

"The money I get for my work here pays for Jack's care and his medical bills. I also approved a raise for Steve and Margie. I suppose I was wrong to do that without talking to you first. I'll change everything back to the way it was." She could make things right with God. Her mother-in-law was another matter.

Clarissa's eyes narrowed. "That's not what I asked. By what authority do you step in and take money that legally belongs to me?"

ASKING FOR A MIRACLE

"Legally you get a large share of the monthly profits from the store. My authority to step in, hire myself, and give raises to employees has nothing to do with that. It comes from the power of attorney Jack gave me. I will return your money."

"Did he know what he was signing? Of course, he didn't. Oh, you are a scheming hussy. I won't let you get away with this. The store is mine if Jack passes before I do. You are conniving to alienate my son and my daughter from me, and to steal this business." Clarissa shook her finger in Carole's direction. "I will see you in court."

Carole couldn't let that happen. It would tear her family apart, and destroy Jack's business. "If you pursue this any further, and take me to court, I will sell the store."

"You can't do that," Clarissa shouted. She jumped from her chair and headed for the door. She was almost there when she turned to face Carole. "Can you?"

"I can persuade Jack to sell it." Carole's heart was in the pit of her stomach. "I will use our share of the money to care for Jack. When I have spent it all, and I will, soon, I will take him to the veteran's hospital over in Wynn City."

"You wouldn't dare." Clarissa gasped. "That's a long way."

"It's a little over two hundred miles, and I would dare. He will get free care there." Carole stood. "I have to get back to my job of selling household appliances."

"Sit down," Clarissa snapped. She went back into Jack's office and sat behind his desk. "I have a few more things to say."

For one brief moment, expectation sprang up inside Carole.

"We can come to some agreement," Clarissa said.

"What kind of agreement?" Carole's hope was tempered by caution.

"I will provide money for your needs, but only if you heed my advice and do my bidding."

BILLIE HOUSTON

Carole didn't have to think twice about such a proposition. *That's blackmail.* "Thanks, but no thanks." She turned. "I have to go now." She hurried through the door and down the hall.

Clarissa's reproachful words followed her. "That's gratitude for you."

Chapter Twenty-Four

June 8, 1975, Sunday Morning

"What are you doing here?" Jack awoke to see Carole sitting in the chair beside his bed. She usually attended church on Sunday morning.

Carole ignored his question. "Did your mother visit you last week?"

"Every day," Jack replied. "Why are you asking when you know she did?"

"There are some things I have to tell you." Carole stared down at her hands folded and resting in her lap.

"I know what you are going to say. Mother is furious with you. She's demanding I make you pay back the money she says you stole from her." Carole lifted her head and looked directly into Jack's eyes. He saw sorrow in their blue depths, and something akin to fear.

"I am paying her back every cent I took. It will wipe out the last of our savings, and that presents another problem."

"Wait a minute." Jack sat up in bed. His love for his wife swept away the last vestige of the self-pity that had been his constant companion for such a long time. "She can't do that. I won't let her."

"In a way she's right. What I did was underhanded and unfair. I shouldn't have done it. All I could think of was getting enough money to care for you, and buy the things Suzanne needed for her graduation."

"You don't have to do this," Jack declared, puzzled as to why she hadn't confided in him sooner. He knew he'd let Carole carry this burden alone far too long.

"I know you don't like me to talk about my Christian faith," Carole paused before going on. "In this case, I must. What I did was wrong in the sight of God. I explained that to Clarissa. I also told her it would bankrupt me to restore what I'd spent. She didn't tell you?"

"All she told me was you are a thief. After that she talked about how I must accept my fate and learn to live with it. She kept saying she would be here for me to lean on." Like a streak of forked lightning, it hit him. "She doesn't want me to walk again." That knowledge was like a knife through his heart. "My own mother wants me to live the rest of my life as an invalid. Why?"

"She has her reasons. She wants to be in control of everything. She said I should go home and take care of my husband and my home." Carole stood and walked across the room before turning to stare at him. "That would make us totally dependent on her. I refused her offer. She told me I would come around, in time. I won't, but I can no longer afford to keep Ralph and Mrs. Dennis. I gave them their notices.

"Clarissa also offered to pay Suzanne's college tuition. To her credit, Suzanne told her no. She's found a job at the Downtown Office Supply. It broke my heart to tell her that right now, college is out of the question. Maybe later—" Her voice cracked on the intake of a sob.

"Why didn't you tell me sooner?" How completely had he failed as a husband and a father?

"I didn't want you to worry." She came back across the room and stood looking down at him. "I have begun making arrangements for you to go to the veteran's hospital in Wynn City. It's a new facility. They offer a variety of services. There will be no charge, and they will take good care of you."

What pampering and sympathy had failed to do, challenge and adversity achieved. "When I leave this room, I will walk out on my good leg and my prosthesis."

"But Jack—"

"I am not going to the hospital in Wynn City." He pounded the bed with his fist. "I'm staying right here, and I am going to walk again, no matter how long it takes."

"I'll help you." Carole clapped her hands together. Her smile was like a bright ray of sunshine. "I can be your coach when you do your physical

therapy." She took one of his hands in both of hers and kissed his fingertips. "I love you, Jack. With God's help we will lick this thing."
"I need all the help I can get."
Carole's smile converted to a frown. "Do you mean that? About accepting help, I mean."
"Every word of it."
"That's a load off my mind." Carole drew a deep, breath. "I've applied for food stamps and welfare benefits. I've also arranged for Otis and Midge to take turns staying with you while I'm working. I am the new clerk at Austin's Department Store."

*****

Carole waited for Jack to object or refuse to go along with her plans. He surprised her.
"Midge has agreed to sit with me? How did you manage that? I was under the impression she hated my guts."
"Midge is having a bad time. Her divorce from Elbert was final last month." She rubbed the back of her neck. "Behave yourself while she's here, and try not to say anything to upset her."
"I thought Elbert was her knight in shining armor." Jack grinned.
"So did Midge until she learned he was having an affair. When she confronted him, he hit her."
Jack smiled.
"Don't laugh. It isn't funny. Midge is devastated."
Carole kicked off her shoes and lay on the bed beside her husband. The bed was narrow. She nestled next to him, and put her arm around his waist. "Forget Midge. Concentrate on making love to your wife."
He moved her arm away. "I'm not up to that. I may never be again."
Does he think—? Obviously, he does. She could soon disabuse him of that silly notion. Two hours later Carole awoke with a start. It took some time for her to remember where she was and what had happened.

BILLIE HOUSTON

She smiled, snuggled closer, and closed her eyes. This is the way it should have been on their wedding night.

Chapter Twenty-Five

June 13, 1975, Friday morning
Every part of Jack's body was afire with intense pain. He sat on the side of his bed and pushed his walker from him. "I'm never going to be able to do this."
Midge dropped into a chair. "You will, if you keep trying."
"Carole should be here with me. She said she would be." He wanted to say much more. He controlled his tongue. Over the last few days, by mutual agreement, a tacit truce existed between him and Midge.
"By the time Carole gets home in the evening, she is bone tired from being on her feet all day. Mornings, when you are rested is the best time to exercise. Stop complaining, and let's have another go at it."
Jack was never 'rested'. Midge was the least sympathetic person he knew. He lay down across his bed. "I can't, I just can't."
"Okay, we will take a fifteen-minute break." Midge agreed, but most ungraciously.
Small wonder four husbands walked out on her.
Jack sat up. The pain was less, but it was still there. Would it ever go away completely?
Otis came into the room. "Otis Thorpe reporting for duty."
"You're early," Midge remarked, as she stood. "You look beat."
"I've been with Ralph. He is giving me some hints about how to take care of our patient."
"Your patient is not doing any more walking until tomorrow," Jack said. The pain in his upper body reduced to a steady ache.
"He's all yours. Maybe you can make him obey doctor's orders." Midge picked up her purse and slung the long strap over her shoulder. "I have

to go. I have an appointment to show a house." She waved her hand in Jack's direction.

Jack's physical discomfort did nothing to improve his frame of mind. "Midge is a slave-driver. I can understand why Elbert left her."

"I brought you some lunch." Otis ignored his remark. "Do you want crackers or cornbread with your chili?"

"You brought me chili for lunch?" Jack lifted his eyebrows in surprise. "Man, it's the middle of June and the temperature has already hit three digits. You expect me to eat chili for lunch?"

"It's the only thing I know how to cook besides cornbread. Maybe you'd rather have milk with that cornbread." A wide grin spread across Otis' face. "You could move to London. It snowed there the second of June, for the first time ever."

Before Jack could answer, Midge came back into the room with Pastor Norman in tow. "Look who I found at the front door. You have a visitor, Jack." She pointed to the chair in the corner. "Sit down, Pastor. See you later. I'm late for an appointment." With another wave of her hand she was out the door again.

Otis jumped to his feet. "Sit here. I was about to go."

His best friend was leaving him with a man he had no desire to be alone with, much less talk to. How lucky Otis was to be able to move about under his own steam. "Where are you off to now?"

Otis said over his shoulder as he went through the door, "Off to the fast-food store to get our lunch." He stopped and turned. "Would you like a burger and fries, Pastor?"

Pastor Norman waved one hand. "No thanks, but a salad would be nice."

"Salad it is." Otis turned, and in an instant was out of sight.

"How have you been, Reverend Norman?" Not that Jack cared.

"Well, thank you, Jack. You don't have to call me reverend. I prefer pastor or preacher. If neither of those suits your taste, you can call me just plain Norman."

"I will call you by your given name, if you have one." This man didn't fit Jack's picture of what a reverend should be. That made him even more uncomfortable and edgy.

"Norman is my given name." A grin spread across the reverend's face. "My full name is Norman Lee Smith."

"I'll call you Smith." A pall of silence fell over the room as Jack searched his mind for something appropriate to say. Anything that would pass for pleasant conversation. He found nothing.

"Do I make you uncomfortable?" Smith came to sit in the chair near Jack's bed.

Jack was too surprised by his blunt question to speak anything but the truth. "You make me very uncomfortable."

"Why?"

"I know you are going to start spewing words from the Bible." If Smith wanted the truth that was what he was going to get. "I don't believe any of that mumbo-jumbo. So, don't waste your time."

Smith shook his head indicating he was in deep thought. "I never before knew anyone who thought the Bible was mumbo jumbo. I'd be interested to hear how you came to that conclusion."

The question caught Jack off-guard. "I—I don't believe in the supernatural."

Smith's brow wrinkled as he heaved a sigh of relief. "What supernatural events in the Bible do you find impossible to believe?"

Jack had never read the Bible. He was most reluctant to admit that. He changed the subject. "What do you think about Ford declaring an end to the Vietnam Era?"

"The end may be declared, but the aftermath will linger on. You didn't answer my question."

The pastor's cryptic answer and bold reminder angered Jack, who was not so careful to keep his tone neutral nor his manner mild. "I have never read the Bible. I would think a man of your standing in the

community and educational background would pay more heed to the events that are going on in the world around him."
"In the future, I will take the time to be more observant of events going on around me."
"I should hope so—"
Before Jack could say more, Smith spoke again. "If you will take the time to peruse the Bible. I'll come to call again in a week or so and we can compare notes."
In the heat of what could pass for a dispute, Jack forgot his pain. "I look forward to your visit." At that time, he'd see who could present the more logical argument.

Chapter Twenty-Six

June 20 1975, Monday Morning
Carole sat in a chair, kicked off her shoes, and put her feet on a footstool. "It's good to have a day off."
Jack lay propped up on several pillows. "It's good to have you to help me with my therapy. Your friend Midge is a slave driver."
"She means well, in her own way." There was no anger in Jack's voice when he spoke of Midge. Could it be that he was beginning to recognize Midge's more sterling qualities?
Jack put that thought to rest when he said, "There is not one ounce of compassion in that woman."
Carole could have argued. What would be the use? "I had a most interesting telephone call last evening. It was from a distant descendant of Oliver P. Duncan, Sr."
"The man who was your father?" Jack moved restlessly in his bed. "What did he have to say?"
"The he is a she. Her name is Margo Hughes. She's a genealogist who keeps an eagle eye on her own family tree. My snooping around, asking questions, came to her attention. She is upset that even a breath of scandal would taint the name of Oliver P. Duncan, Sr., and displeased with me for, and I quote, 'stirring up such a stink over what was no more than vicious gossip.'"
"I'm sure you set her straight."
Carole opened her mouth to say, 'God has taught me'. She closed her lips before the words could escape, took a breath, and started over. "I didn't bother. I have learned that the past is not important. Now is. This moment is alive, and it's mine. The future that lies ahead is a promise

that I can shape, to some degree, from day to day, as I continue my life's journey." She sat up and put her feet on the floor. "I have things to do."
"Wait, don't go."
Jack smiled. She hadn't seen him do that in a long time.
"From whom did you acquire such words of wisdom?"
"It's a long story." Carole sat again and put her feet back on the stool. "Why do you ask?"
"It gives me hope that someday you will forgive me for my past indiscretions."
"I have forgiven you." She could, at last, say that and know it to be true. "I have wished for such a long time to hear those words, and believe you mean them. Now, tell me that long story."
Heavenly Father, give me the right words to say. Carole drew a long breath, and began. "I grew up feeling something was missing in my life. I had no father, no sisters or brothers, not even any cousins, aunts or uncles. I felt life had slighted me. Instead of pitying myself, I should have counted my blessings.
"You didn't know the circumstances," Jack protested. "You were only a child."
"I became an adult. No. I should say I grew up. Sometimes I think I am still a long way from being an adult. When I learned Aunt Effie was really my mother, all those old memories came flooding back. I had no reason to, but I blamed her for what I considered my pitiful plight. I deserted you and Suzanne and went searching for some noble, non-existent father who never was, except in my own mind. If I had been here, with you and Suzanne, you would never have been on that highway that night, you would never—" She put her head on the chair arm and wept bitterly.
"Are you blaming yourself for my accident?" Jack's voice dropped to a growl. "You must never do that. Darling please, stop your crying and get on with your story."

ASKING FOR A MIRACLE

Carole stifled her sobs, lifted her head, and dried her eyes with her dress hem. "I'm not sure you'd care to hear the rest of my story." She didn't want to make him angry, not after he had called her darling. Maybe, despite her many mistakes, there was still hope for her marriage.

"Let me be the judge of that. Speak."

"I have rededicated my life to serving Jesus. When I did that, I put the past behind me. I came to realize that being a Christian is a daily process. I want to forget my past mistakes and live each day, each moment, for my Savior. I learned that, along with what true forgiveness is, from reading my Bible, and listening, really listening, to Pastor Norman's sermons. When you can walk again—"

"Wait a minute." Jack sat up in bed. His smile disappeared to be replaced with a deep scowl. "I may walk again, but I will never be a normal man again. I am not going to grow another leg. Stop asking for a miracle."

"I'm not asking that you grow another leg, but if we have faith—"

"Don't start, Carole. I am willing to accept that you have deep religious convictions. By the same token, you must accept that I am a semi-invalid and always will be. Why won't you grant me the right to accept my condition and deal with it as I see fit?"

"You are as much a man as you ever were. Jack, please be reasonable. Sweetheart—"

"You, who are asking for a miracle, want *me* to be reasonable?" He folded his arms across his chest, and glared at her. "Maybe it would be best if you did put me in that new veteran's hospital with all the other scrap heaps of humanity, and forget me."

"I never thought I would say this to you, Jackson Garner." She stood and slipped her feet into her shoes. "You are a spiritual coward. You are afraid to believe, you are afraid to hope, you are even afraid to try. I'll see what I can do about getting you into that veteran's hospital." She walked from the room without looking back or saying another word.

BILLIE HOUSTON

*****

In a matter of minutes she returned. "You have a visitor." Without waiting for his response, she turned and hurried toward the door.
Norman Smith smiled at her as she sped past him.
Carole didn't return his smile.
"I must have offended your wife." Pastor Norman sat in the chair near Jack's bed. "If I did, it was unintentional."
"She's not mad at you. She's mad at me. She just let me have it with both barrels. She says I am a coward, afraid to believe, or hope, or even try." A stab of pain knifed through him. "She did agree to look into sending me to that new veteran's hospital."
"Are you?" Smith leaned forward and studied Jack's face. "Afraid to believe or hope or try?"
Was he? "I never considered what I feel to be fear."
"Maybe it's time you did." Smith leaned back in his chair and waited for Jack's response.
A multitude of conflicting emotions swept through him. "I need some time to think about this." He sorted through his thoughts, one by one. He *was* afraid to believe. "How can I place my trust in some supreme being I can't see?"
"You exercise something called faith, which is no more than choosing to believe what we want to be will happen."
"Are you telling me if I choose to believe I can lead a normal life again, it will come to pass?"
"I am telling you if you choose to believe you can't lead a normal life again, you won't." Smith tented his fingers, placed his forefingers to his lips, and waited.
After several minutes, Jack spoke. "I can't bring myself to trust a God I can't see. I don't understand how you can."
"I feel Him. He speaks to me through His Spirit."

"Spirits can't speak." Or can they? A recollection, buried deep and long forgotten, danced like some evil dervish, through Jack's memory. His mother sat around a table in a semi-dark room, holding hands with three other women. Her words ran through his little-boy brain, terrifying him, causing him to push himself farther into the shadows of his hiding place under the stairway. "Do your magic, Agatha. Summon up an evil spirit, Satan himself, if he is available."

An eerie voice ricocheted from the dark recesses of the room. Jack put his hands over his ears, slipped from his shadowy nook, and ran for his room. Was his mother in league with the devil? That was a chilling thought.

Over the next few years, he'd convinced himself it was all a fraud, another one of his mother's crazy tricks to promote her latest cause of communicating with the dead. Eventually that memory slipped to the back of his mind, gone, forgotten—so he thought—until now. Was it all an invention of his imagination?

"Will you pray with me?" Smith bowed his head. "Let's test your theory."

"Wait a minute preacher." Jack lifted one hand. "I told you, I don't believe in spirits."

"Is it disbelief or is it fear that makes you afraid to call out to the Holy Spirit?"

Jack was more than afraid. He was terrified. His mind acknowledged an anxiety he had harbored since childhood, and never admitted to a living soul. "Suppose some evil spirit answers? I don't want any part of evil spirits."

Smith man bowed his head. "Neither does God. Let's pray."

Jack bridled his irritation and followed suit. Maybe some spirit would take him and end his misery.

Smith spoke in a soft and confident voice. He could have been talking to a dear friend, someone wise and loving. "Heavenly Father we come to you with grateful hearts and humble spirits..."

Jack's thoughts wandered as he waited for that wedge of fear to lodge in his chest. It never arrived. He wanted to raise his head and call a halt to these proceedings. Some power stronger than Jack Garner stopped him. A calm replaced his uncertainty. Quiet fell over the room. *What is happening to me?* He pulled his mind back to Smith's prayer.

"Help Jack to feel your presence. Take away his fear and doubt. Bless him and give him the strength, both physical and spiritual, to try again..."

Once more Jack's thoughts strayed. He didn't want to be afraid, or have no hope, he wanted to believe and try again, over and over again. He needed help. He knew he couldn't do this alone.

Smith laid his hand on Jack's arm and said a resounding "Amen," before lifting his head and smiling. "Lest I forget to tell you, I have made a point of keeping abreast with current events. I can now converse with some knowledge about our president falling down a stairway in Austria, the Soviet Space Program, the reopening of the Suez Canal—"

"I'm impressed." Jack had just experienced something transforming and awesome. "We can talk about all those things later." Now he must rest, and think, and try to make sense of the confusion inside him.

"I will leave you with your thoughts. God bless you." Smith smiled as he stood and walked away.

Chapter Twenty-Seven

July 4, 1975, Friday Evening
Carole sat in the glider on her patio and watched the town's annual display of bursting fireworks light up the night sky. The smell of barbeque drifted from the backyard of the house two doors down. Chatter of children mingled with the sounds of adults laughing and talking while families celebrated the holiday. Suzanne was with Cindy and her family. It was the Fourth of July, and she sat alone in her back yard, bone weary and worried sick over Jack's worsening condition. He lived with pain, even though at four-hour intervals through each day and night, she gave him doses of pain medication. If and when he recovered, would he be addicted to the drugs he took?

She wanted to put her trust in God and believe this was all a part of His grand scheme, but that was becoming increasingly difficult. She tried to stay cheerful in Jack's presence. However, his negative attitude, and constant complaining of pain, were wearing her down. Maybe she should send him away.

She could never do that. What was she thinking?

She went into the house, locked the door, and tiptoed into Jack's room. He slept, tossing and turning, and mumbling in his sleep.

She sat in a chair, turned on the lamp beside her, and reached for her Bible. A low voice spoke inside her head. *Open my Holy Book, child, and read.*

She let the Bible fall open, closed her eyes, placed her finger on a verse on the middle of the page, and read:

Let this mind be in you which was also in Christ Jesus: Who being in the form of God thought it not robbery to be equal with God: But made himself of no reputation, and took upon him the form of a servant, and was made in the likeness of men: And being found in the fashion of a man, he humbled himself, and became obedient unto death, even the death of the cross. Philippians 2: 5-8.

Tears blinded her as she closed the Bible and laid it on the table beside her chair. If this perfect man Christ Jesus could so unquestionably obey His Father, humble himself and die on a cross for her sins, who was she to question the path God chose to lead her down? She was ashamed and repentant. She whispered, "Father forgive me."

Jack stirred. "Carole?" His eyes opened. "What's wrong?"

She replied with the question uppermost in her mind. "Does suffering have its own reward?"

"What are you talking about?" He grimaced as he tried to pull himself up in bed.

"Be still," Carole snapped. She struggled to her feet and moved toward the bed. "I was thinking of how Jesus suffered before he died."

"I hope he wasn't in a car accident." Jack put his hand over his mouth and yawned.

"Don't be facetious." Carole sat on the side of the bed. "He was nailed to a wooden cross, and lifted up to hang there until He died. Roman soldiers pierced his side with a spear. He hung on that cross for hours. The reward for his suffering was salvation for whosoever will believe He is God's son and confess Him publicly."

*****

Suffering Jack understood. "So you think my suffering has a reward somewhere down the line?"

"I think you can use it to the glory of God, if you so choose."

"You never give up, do you?" In the light of day Jack might have rebuked Carole for that remark. In the dark of night with fireworks intermittently exploding in loud bursts, he had a desire to know more of this story his wife believed in so completely. "Tell me about your Jesus."

ASKING FOR A MIRACLE

Carole spoke in a slow, soft voice. She began with the birth of Jesus, and then told of Joseph and Mary's flight to Egypt.

The pain in Jack's leg was severe. He fought to keep his attention on what Carol said.

"Jack, are you all right?"

"Yes," he replied. "Go on."

Carole continued, telling of the twelve-year-old Jesus in the temple confounding the temple leaders with his knowledge and understanding. She talked for some time, telling of Jesus' baptism and ministry—how he healed the sick, raised the dead, and cast out demons—

"Whoa," Jack interrupted. "I don't want to hear about demons. That's getting too far over into the occult."

"What is it with you and the occult?" Carole asked.

"You wouldn't understand." He didn't want to talk of his long-standing irrational fear, or speak about his newly-resurrected boyhood memory.

Carole jumped to her feet and walked across the room before turning to face him. "Why didn't I know it before?"

"Know what?"

"Don't you see?" She came back across the room and sat on the bed once more. "That's our problem. It has been all along."

"You lost me somewhere between your getting up and sitting down again." Jack shook his head, trying to find some connection between the subject being discussed and Carole's last words. "Your religion is no problem for me. I accept your right to believe. I—"

"You said I wouldn't understand. That's our problem. We are afraid to trust and confide in each other. How do you know I wouldn't understand?"

"I know you, that's why."

"I don't think you do. Maybe you never have." Tears filled her eyes. "I don't know you either. Don't you think it's time we got acquainted?"

The truth of her words hit him like the exploding firecrackers that echoed through the night. "Where do we start?"
"I have always heard the best place to begin is at the beginning." Carole moved to the chair beside Jack's bed. "For me, 'we' began when I first saw you."
"We were kids in high school." Jack smiled. He hadn't done that in a long time. "You were a freshman. I was a senior."
"We shared a study hall. I spent a lot of my study time looking at you and daydreaming. You didn't know I existed. When did 'we' begin for you?"
Jack's memory travelled backward in time to the night he met his wife for the first time. "The night of Marty Stillwell's 1947 New Year's Eve party. The moment he introduced you, I knew you would be an important person in my life."
"That long?" Carole's eyes opened wide. "That was almost thirty years ago."
"Twenty-seven years, to be exact. You wore a fuzzy pink sweater and a circular black skirt. I was smitten with you from the first moment I saw you."
"You didn't act smitten." Carole leaned forward and touched his hand with her finger tips. "You asked for my telephone number and then waited three weeks to call. Why?"
"I was scared." Why, indeed, did he wait so long to admit his fears to Carole, and to himself?
"Scared of what?"
Jack spoke slowly, as he sorted through old, half-forgotten memories "I was scared of the way I felt about you." He paused, trying to collect his thoughts. "I was afraid you'd refuse to go out with me." *I may as well admit the rest.* "I was afraid of forming a close relationship with any woman. That fear battled with my desire to claim you for my own." A voice in the back of his head prodded, *Tell the truth and shame the devil.* "My relationship with my mother colored my view of all women." Pain

mixed with the fear. Would Carole ridicule his soul-baring admission?
"I'm tired. I need to rest."
"I understand." Carole took his hand in hers and squeezed it. "Each of us is a victim of our upbringing. All through my childhood I believed I had been cheated out of a family. Now, looking back, I realize Aunt Effie *was* my family, and she was enough. Even my search for my father wasn't in vain. I have connected with my distant cousins."
"I am glad you found them." Relief, along with understanding, lifted Jack's spirits. "We were young then. We knew so little about life. We are older now, and wiser. We can cope with our problems."
"Would you mind if I said a prayer thanking God for our new-found understanding?" Her fingers laced through his as she held on tight. "I won't if you'd rather I didn't."
"I would be pleased to have my wife pray over me. After that, you and I have much talking to do." Jack bowed his head.
Carole followed suit, and spoke in soft, sweet tones.
"Father God, accept my gratitude for Your many blessings. Thank you for leading Jack and me to this new understanding. Help us to re-build our marriage. This time let it be in accordance with Your will. Help us to be open and honest with each other. Help me to be an example to this man I love so much. Heal his body, Lord. Make him well again." Sobs shook through her. After some struggle, she whispered, "In Christ's name I pray, Amen"
Jack lifted his head. "Now for that talk." He pulled a facial tissue from the box on his nightstand, and wiped his eyes.

Chapter Twenty-Eight

August 3, 1975, Sunday Noon

Carole was out of the church and walking toward her car when Ralph Warren caught up to her. "Pastor Norman preached a wonderful sermon this morning."

"It was indeed," Carole agreed.

Ralph asked, "How is Jack doing?"

"He's no longer taking pain medication." Carole slowed her pace. "The doctors say there is no reason he should not lead a normal life again with the aid of a prosthesis." She moved to a tall oak tree, and stood in its shade. "Even though the constant pain is gone, trying to walk on his temporary prosthesis is still painful."

"Jack needs some faith in himself, and in God." Ralph stiffened his arm, propped one hand against the tree and stared down at her. "His negative attitude hinders his recovery."

"Don't you think I know that? Don't you think I've said as much to Jack at least a hundred times? Nothing I say makes any difference. Maybe I should give up and stop pushing him."

"You must never give up." Ralph's smile invited confidence. "I have been praying for Jack. God has put it in my heart to do more than pray. I have an idea. Is Otis at church this morning?"

"He's over there." Carole pointed. "Talking to Deacon Maxwell."

"Stay put. I'll get him." Ralph sprinted across the churchyard. Carole watched as he took Otis' arm and led him toward her.

"What's up?" Otis asked as they reached the shade of the tree.

"Ask Ralph." Carole shrugged. "This little pow-wow is his idea."

Ralph shoved his hands into his pockets. "We have to get Jack out of that bed and living again."

"How do you propose to do that?" Otis scratched the side of his head. "I've done everything from shaming him to begging him. He turns a deaf ear to all my pleas."

"I keep telling you, he's given up hope." Carole leaned against the tree. "He's convinced he will be a cripple for the rest of his life. I hate to admit it, but so am I. It would take a miracle to give him hope again."

"Let's ask God for that miracle," Ralph said. "Then, believing He will grant it, go to work helping to make it happen."

How many times had she believed, and been disappointed? She believed her mother was her aunt. She wasn't. She believed Jack was faithful to his marriage vows. He wasn't. She believed her father would be a fine, decent man. He wasn't. *"Sometimes God says no."*

"We never know until we ask." Otis took his handkerchief from his pocket and mopped perspiration from his brow. "How do I go about helping God, past praying for Jack?"

"We make him walk on his temporary prosthesis every day until he accepts it as a way of life." Ralph loosened his tie. "Are you guys with me?"

Otis nodded agreement. Then asked, "Do you have a plan?"

Carole shrugged. "It's worth a try." This time she wouldn't be disappointed when they failed.

Ralph stuck his tie in his suit coat pocket "I do. Let's get out of this heat and go somewhere we can talk. My family and I are headed for the Blue Goose Restaurant for lunch. Meet us there. We can find a quiet corner and talk over this situation." He waved as he walked away. "See you there."

*****

The Blue Goose was cool and dark, and a welcome change from the heat outside.

ASKING FOR A MIRACLE

Once Carole's eyes adjusted to the dimmer light, she saw Ralph waving from a back booth. She waved back, and took Otis' arm. "This way."
Ralph and his wife were seated on one side of the booth. Grace was a beautiful woman, tall, slender, and graceful.
Carole slid into the bench on the other side. "Where are your children?"
Grace looked at Ralph before saying, "They went home with Grandma and Granddad Warren."
Ralph shook his head. "There should be a law against doting grandparents. By the time we get home with them tonight, they will on a sugar high, and impossible to calm and get into bed."
Grace reminded him, "Grandma and Granddad are your mama and daddy."
"They were strict parents. Something happened along the way to change them into adoring grandparents who spoil John and Rachel rotten."
A waitress appeared with menus. As she walked away, Otis tucked his napkin under his chin. "I'm waiting to hear about your plan to help God work a miracle."
"All we have to do is believe and keep working." Ralph took a sip from his glass of water. "We do the work and trust God to provide the miracle."
Otis leaned forward, concern written in the lines of his face and distress darkening his eyes. "I'm with you buddy. I'll do whatever it takes to help Jack."
"Jack's not easily persuaded." Carole hated bursting Ralph's bubble of hope. He needed to realize the improbability of his plan ever bringing about the desired results. "He has no faith in God."
Ralph replied, "We have faith. If we have enough faith, and work without ceasing, God will hear us, and answer our request."
Carole had more doubts than faith. "I'm willing to work and pray for Jack's healing." What could it hurt to try?

BILLIE HOUSTON

"Great." Ralph bowed his head and reached across the table. "Let's hold hands as I ask God to bless our food. Then we can get down to business."

Chapter Twenty-Nine

August 7, 1975, Thursday Noon

"Thank you for coming." Carole reached across the small space that separated them and caught Midge's hand. They sat at a tiny table tucked away in a far corner of Tillie's Tea Room. "I need to talk to you."

"I have some things to tell you too." Midge squeezed her friend's hand. "You first."

"It's about Jack."

Midge smiled. "Why am I not surprised?" Her smile vanished as quickly as it had appeared. "Forgive me. You should be concerned about your husband. Is he still insisting you send him to the veteran's hospital?"

"Yes. But not as often. Ralph has come up with a plan to get him to do his exercises, change his attitude, and eventually get his life back to normal again. I said I'd go along with his idea, but the more I think about it, the more I think it will be a waste of time." Carole took a bite of her sandwich.

"Otis is very gung-ho about it working. It sounds like a good plan to me" Midge stirred her salad with her fork.

"Otis?" Carole questioned. "When did you see Otis? What did he tell you?"

"Oops." Midge dropped her fork, and slapped her hand over her mouth, then removed it slowly. "Now that the cat is out of the bag, I may as well 'fess up. I've been seeing Otis for some time now. Things have become serious between us. That's what I wanted to talk to you about."

"You and Otis?" This would never work. She had to put a stop to it now. "When did this happen?"

"I got to really know Otis when he and I were babysitting your husband." Midge squirmed in her seat. "He's a fine man, not like anyone I ever met before."

"Midge, honey, I love you like a sister." There was no way she could stand by and see her friend make another mistake. "You can't be serious. The two of you are as different as day and night."

"In our case, opposites attract." Midge leaned across the table and smiled. "We are going to be married Christmas Eve. Pastor Norman is performing the ceremony after Wednesday night services. I'm hoping you will be my matron of honor."

Carole's heart thumped against her ribs. She didn't want to offend her dearest friend, neither could she let this chance to talk some sense into her head to slip away. "Are you sure you're not marrying Otis on the rebound?"

"I am not. I love Otis."

"Give yourself some time to be sure."

"I don't need any more time. I am going to marry the man I love, and I'm going to do it on the eve of Jesus' birthday."

Carole could have said so many things. She didn't. "Just remember, nothing is ever what we think it's going to be."

"I know, I know" With a wave of her hand, Midge dismissed Carole's words of warning, and changed the subject. "Otis said you were going to ask me to help with Ralph's plan to rehabilitate Jack. You know I will. Otis and I have talked about how we must commit completely to praying for him, even as we work to see that he exercises and walks each day. We must encourage him and pray for his salvation."

"What has happened to you?" Carole was surprised and a little envious. "You and Otis talked?" If only she and Jack had started out with that kind of relationship. "I haven't heard you talk like this since—I don't know when."

"When we talked to Pastor Norman, Otis and I rededicated our lives to serving Jesus."

ASKING FOR A MIRACLE

"You did? Both of you? That's wonderful." Once again, envy reared its ugly head. How much it would mean to her to have a Christ-centered marriage. She pushed her plate toward Midge. "Have one of my tea cakes."
"No thanks, I don't want to be a fat bride." Midge pushed her half-finished salad from her. "Have you told Jack about our plan?"
"Not yet. I'm going to break the news to him tonight over dinner."
Midge glanced at her watch and stood. "I have to go. Good luck belling the cat." She grabbed her handbag and headed for the door.

*****

The nearer the time came to tell Jack of Ralph's plan, the more doubt slipped in around Carole's assurance. What if he refuses? What if this destroyed everything they'd done over the past few weeks to bring them closer together? Maybe they should call the whole thing off. She stuck her head through the door to Jack's room. "Do you mind if I have dinner with you tonight?"
"Please yourself," Jack said, with indifference.
Carole bit her lip to keep back a caustic reply. She went to the kitchen and returned with a rolling cart holding two filled plates, iced tea, bread, and dessert. She set Jack's dinner on his tray, before pulling the cart near the rocker and sitting down. "I am going to ask God to bless this food."
"Make it fast." Jack sat up and viewed his plate with distaste.
Carole bowed her head and closed her eyes. The thought came like an epiphany. There is something of more importance that must be set straight between them before she spoke to him of Ralph's plan.
Her breath caught in her throat. Why didn't she realize it before? She had known, for a long time. Knowing the truth and facing hard facts were two different things. "Dear Lord, bless this food to the nourishment of our bodies and forgive us of our sins. Give me the courage to face this showdown and to accept the results. Amen"

"May I eat now?" Jack reached for his fork.
Carole nodded her consent. "I have something to say to you, something I should have said on our wedding night."
Jack laid his fork on his tray. "I don't want to hear it."
Carole's first instinct was to storm from the room. She had done that so often before. Not this time. "You have no choice. You are a captive audience. You can't leave, and I refuse to go until I say what is on my mind and in my heart."
"Have your say." Jack leaned back on his pillows. "Then go."
"It's sad how a silence between two people can fester like an open sore. Given time, it spreads like a cancer until it eats away understanding, and intimacy."
"What are you talking about?" Jack wrinkled his brow.
"I'm talking about us." She pointed to him, and then to herself. "You and me." At least now she had his attention. "You and I met, and by chance we fell in love. Our wedding night was a disaster. We had the choice of remaining silent and letting that painful incident grow and rankle, or as agonizing as it would have been, talking about it and attempting to repair the damage. We were young and didn't know how to go about mending the harm and hurt. It grew and ate into what we felt for each other. We have never been close. We are older now. We understand that being in love is one thing, staying in love is another. I would like for us to work toward repairing years of neglect and damage."
"Do you think that's possible?" He stared at her with the strangest look in his eyes.
"With God anything is possible." She gritted her teeth and waited for his angry reply. After several seconds of strained silence, she added, "I love you, Jack. I want to find a way to grow close to you, and share my thoughts and hopes, and even my disappointments, with you. I want us to be intimate in every sense of the word."
"It's been a long time since I felt any emotion at all. I'm dead inside."

ASKING FOR A MIRACLE

"Would you like to be born again?"

"I can't go on this way. I can't do this by myself." Tears rolled down his cheeks. She had never seen him cry before.

Her heart hurt. What he felt was pain of the worst kind—the spiritual pain of a lost man. "I can show you a more excellent way. Will you allow me to do that?"

He bowed his head as tears spilled from his eyes, and rolled down his cheeks. "Please do before I sink forever into this sea of hopelessness."

She moved Jack's tray and sat beside him. "I never loved you more than I do at this moment."

Chapter Thirty

August 7, 1975
Thursday Night

Jack wiped his eyes with the end of his sheet. He had come to a dead end. His life was a burden he could no longer bear. Carole's sweet words lifted his spirit. "You really mean that, don't you? You really do love me."
"With every beat of my heart." She laid her hand over her left breast. "More and more with each passing day."
"I love you, too." He hesitated, fearful of breaking the magic of the spell that was spinning between them. "I... I.... Never mind."
"Yes, mind. That's our basic problem. Don't you see?" She took his hand in hers. "We have built a wall of silence between us. The only way to tear it down is to speak our hearts."
"I know you want to talk to me about your Jesus. I will listen because I am desperate, clutching at straws. Before you begin, there is something I must confess to you." He hesitated. "It's so foolish. It's childish. I don't—"
"Talk to me, Jack." She dropped his hand. "Tell me. I need to know." Her expression was a mixture of compassion and fear. Did she think he was going to confess another indiscretion?
"It's about an incident that occurred many years ago." He took her hand in his, turned it over, and kissed her upturned palm before telling her, in halting terms, his experience with seeing his mother's séance. He ended by saying, "I told you it was foolish, but I can't rid myself of the fear of the occult and evil spirits."
"Have you been reading this?" Carole asked, as she picked up the Bible that lay on Jack's nightstand.
"A little, now and then," Jack admitted. "Most of it I don't understand."

"May I read you a passage of scripture?"
"If you must." That same old fear that came each time he faced spirits and the occult hit him with hurricane force.
"I must." She opened the Bible. "This passage is from Matthew, chapter eight.

> *And when he (Jesus) was come out to the other side of the country of Gergesenes, there met him two (men) possessed with devils, coming out of the tombs, exceeding fierce, so that no man might pass that way.*
>
> *And behold, they cried out saying, what have we to do with thee, Jesus, thou Son of God? Art thou come hither to torment us before the time?*
>
> *And there was a good way off from them an herd of many swine feeding.*
>
> *So the devils besought him, saying, If thou cast us out, suffer us to go away into the herd of swine.*
>
> *And he said unto them. Go. And when they were come out, they went into the herd of swine: and, behold, the whole herd ran violently down a steep place into the sea, and perished in the waters. Matthew 8:28-34.*

"Those devils knew who Jesus was. They called him the Son of God." So many conflicting questions chased themselves around inside Jack's head. "I don't understand how Jesus could be a man and God at the same time."
"He was born of a virgin. He was God in a human body. Thus, he was both man and God. He was tempted just like you and me. Yet during the thirty-three years of his life, he never sinned. Because he was perfect, he could offer himself as a sacrifice on the cross for the sins of

the world. Three days after his horrible death, he rose from the grave to live eternally. He offers that same eternal life to all who believe on him and repent."

An emotion he had never felt before tugged at Jack's heartstrings. If Jesus could cast out devils, maybe God's son could help him. "Those devils knew Jesus. They called him the Son of God."

"They also knew He had the power to destroy them." Carole lifted her hands with her palms out. "Jesus sent the Holy Spirit into the world after he ascended to heaven. That Spirit speaks to the hearts of lost souls and helps believers share a closer walk with God."

"I have walked in darkness for such a long time." Jack grabbed both of Carole's extended hands and held on tight. "Help me to step into the glorious light of salvation. Pray for this lost soul."

She held onto his hands and bowed her head. "Gracious Heavenly Father, send the light of The Holy Spirit into Jack's heart. Let that Spirit shine and show him the way to salvation."

Jack interrupted her with an impassioned cry, "Jesus, I believe." His voice dropped to a whisper. "Forgive me for my many sins. Welcome me into your kingdom as one of your children." A peace such as he had never known flooded his heart. Light shone into the dark places of his soul. He was set free from the fear that had stalked him since childhood.

Carole pulled her hands from his tight grasp, clasped them together, and looked heavenward. "Thank you, Jesus."

Chapter Thirty-One

September 1, 1975, Monday Morning

The next few weeks passed in a commotion of always-behind and hurry-hurry. Carole stopped trying to plan ahead, and faced each day as it came. Jack began to be cooperative. He practiced walking daily on his temporary prosthesis, although he found it difficult to keep his balance, and extremely painful. He showed little improvement. Carole's heart broke to see him in so much agony. She always encouraged him to hang on. "Things will get better if we put our trust in Our Savior." As time passed, she began to have little whispers of doubt.

She voiced her thoughts to Midge. Her friend refused to even talk about having doubts. "Jack, with God's help, will get through this."

"That's easy for you to say." Weariness like a knife stabbed between Carole's shoulder blades. She was so tired, both spiritually and physically. "Jack's not the man you love." She was immediately repentant. "Forgive me. I didn't mean that. I don't know how I would make it without you and Otis, and Ralph and Grace."

"It's all right." Midge patted Carole's hand. "I understand. No, I can't understand completely, because I haven't walked in your footsteps. But I know this is hard for you."

"God is punishing me for my years of waywardness. I have so many problems and I don't know how to deal with them. How did I go so wrong?" Tears filled Carole's eyes.

Midge moved to put a comforting arm around Carole's shoulders. "Do you remember Pastor Norman's sermon last Sunday about casting our cares on Jesus because he cares for us?"

Carole did recall. *Casting all your cares upon him; for He careth for you. 1ˢᵗ Peter 5:7.* "I heard, but I didn't heed."

"Whoever said our Christian journey would be easy?" Midge gave Carole an affectionate squeeze before dropping her hand to her side. "Heed that promise now. Claim it, and move forward with helping Jack heal, both physically and spiritually."

"I am so grateful for you as a friend," Carole said. "I'm proud of the way you are growing spiritually."

"I draw my strength from God, and from Otis. He's changed since Jack's accident. I know this has been terrible for you, and for Jack. But in a backhanded way, it's a blessing for Otis and for me. It was God's way of drawing us both back to Him and bringing us together. In a way it's been a blessing to Jack, too. He would never have found Jesus as his savior if he hadn't hit rock bottom with no way to go but up. When Jesus offered him that hand up, he took it."

"When did you get so wise?" Carole was both surprised and troubled. How could her best friend say her husband's horrific accident was a good thing? "Is your advice to dump all my problems in Jesus' lap and forget about them?"

"I'm saying let Him help you by sharing your burdens. That's what I'm trying to do."

"You have burdens to bear?" Carole's voice lifted in surprise. "Like what?"

Midge met Carole's steady gaze. "My past for one thing. I feel unworthy of Otis. Another is the regret that I didn't find him sooner. He loves children. I'm sure he'd like to have a family. I can't give him that."

How selfish I have been. "Have you talked to Otis about these things?"

"I talk to Otis about everything. One of the things I love about him is that he listens to me." Midge ran her fingers through her hair. "Enough about me."

"Midge, do you think Jack's accident is a punishment?"

ASKING FOR A MIRACLE

"Sometimes," Midge answered after a moment. "If we keep doing horrible things that hurt other people. But when you said Jack was suffering because of your—what was it? Oh, yes, waywardness. No, I don't believe God works that way."

A slow smile spread across Carole's face before she burst out in laughter. She grabbed Midge in a bear hug. "What would I do without you?"

"You would be a bigger mess than you are now." Midge returned the hug before pushing away. "We have work to do. Let's get busy."

"You're a slave driver." Carole thought for a while before saying, "Maybe you're right. We can't expect our Christian walk to be easy, but we can rest in the knowledge that Jesus walks with us."

*****

September 1, 1975
Monday Evening

Jack would always remember Labor Day, 1975 as the first day he walked on his temporary prosthesis without wanting to cry out in pain. It hurt, but the intense agony was reduced to a throbbing ache. He was able to walk to the living room and back to his bed.

Carole was ecstatic. "Look how far you walked. Praise the Lord. Oh, Jack, this is wonderful."

"The pain is lessening." He sat on his bed and began the process of removing his prosthesis.

Carole jumped from her chair. "Let me do that."

"I can manage, thank you." Six weeks ago, he would have been angered by her offer to help. Not anymore. So much had changed since he let go and let God have His way. He removed his prosthesis easily and without help.

Jack kept a log of how far he walked each day, and listed a number from one to ten to register his pain level. He looked forward to the time he could stop this tedious recording, and be fitted for a permanent prosthesis. As he wrote, he noted the words under the date of

September first. Labor Day. He looked at his wife. "Do you remember where we were last Labor Day?"

"I remember." Carole nodded. "So much has happened in one short year, and so much has changed. I'm not the same person I was a year ago."

"I've changed, too. One year has transformed my life completely. God has turned me around and set my feet on a different path." His grin widened. "Maybe I should say He set my *foot* on a different path. How sad that God had to maim my body to get my attention. Never again will I be the proud man I once was. I have a crippled body, but my spirit is whole. Of the two, the latter is more important."

Carole put away the temporary prosthesis and came to sit beside him. "I have never felt closer to you than I do now. I feel your nearness as never before."

Jack felt the same, both physically and spiritually. He took her hand in his. "Tell me about your day."

"It was just another day. I did have a most interesting conversation with Midge." She told him what Midge said about his accident being a back-handed blessing. "She credits you with bringing her and Otis together."

"Otis asked me to be his best man at their wedding," Jack said. "I told him yes. My prayer is I will be able to stand by his side when Pastor Norman performs the ceremony." For the first time in a long time, hope stirred inside him. "With God's help, I will be able to do that."

"You will be there by his side, I know." Carole stood and looked at her watch. "Ralph will be here soon. I'll make fresh coffee."

Jack had come to look forward to Ralph's visits. He drew spiritual strength from this man who had become a good friend. God did indeed move in mysterious ways.

Chapter Thirty-Two

November 27, 1975, Thursday Morning

Midge helped Carole put an extension in the dining room table. "Will Suzanne be here for Thanksgiving dinner?"

"Yes, and she's bringing a guest." Carole helped Midge push the extension and the table together.

"Is Cindy home from college?" Midge finished her task and stepped back

"It's not Cindy." Carole grimaced. "It's a boyfriend." She covered the table with the crocheted tablecloth Aunt Effie had used every Thanksgiving since she could remember.

"Are you sure you want to use this tablecloth?" Midge straightened the corners on her side of the table. "What's this boy's name?

Carole positioned a thin sheet of plastic over the tablecloth. "This should take care of it. And if it doesn't, what good is it if I can't use it?"

"None. Are Ralph and Grace bringing their children? Tell me more about Suzanne's new boyfriend."

"They are, even though Ralph's parents wanted to take them to North Carolina to spend Thanksgiving with Ralph's sister. They are adorable children. I rented two highchairs for them to sit in during dinner."

"Did you rent a high chair for Suzanne's boyfriend?" Midge did have a way of putting Carole on the defensive.

"Save your droll wit for someone who appreciates it. Why would I rent a high chair for a grown man?"

Midge, belligerent as only she could be, retorted, "I'm not going to shut up until you tell me all you know about him."

"You are relentless." Carole didn't know anything about him and that was the problem. "It's someone she met at work. She's only known him a short time. He's probably some pimple-faced stock boy. You be nice to him." Carole shook her finger in Midge's direction "Do you hear?" Midge had a way of getting under people's skin when she chose.

"I'll be good. I promise." Midge counted on her fingers. "There's you and Jack, Otis and me, Suzanne and Anonymous, Ralph and Grace, Steve and Margie—"

Carole stopped her. "Steve and Margie won't be here. They are spending Thanksgiving with Steve's children."

"You're kidding me." Midge opened her eyes wide surprise. "Margie hates Steve's kids."

"I know. I hope and pray Margie behaves herself."

"Let's cross our fingers." Midge pulled her brows together in a frown. "Where do you want Clarissa to sit? Not next to me, please."

"Clarissa says she's not coming," Carole said after she heaved a sigh of guilty relief. "She wanted to go with Steve and Margie. Steve told her no, and she's been sulking ever since. She tried to badger Margie into refusing to go. I am happy to say, Margie stood up to her. Now she says she's not going anywhere for Thanksgiving, but who knows? She may show up."

"Should I set a place for her?"

Carole thought a while before saying, "No. If she puts in an appearance, we will set a place for her then."

"Not by me, if you value our friendship." Midge headed for the kitchen.

*****

November 27, 1975
Thursday Evening
Jack sat in the middle of the couch and laid his arms along its back. "It's been a wonderful day. The dinner was delicious. Who made that Dutch apple pie?"

"Grace did. Wasn't it scrumptious? I asked for her recipe." Carole hesitated before asking, "Are you disappointed that Clarissa didn't come?"

The old Jack would have hidden behind his masculine bravado and said no. This was a new Jack. He said, with a note of sadness in his voice, "I am. I know she can be totally obnoxious, but she *is* my mother." How good it felt to be open and honest about his emotions, and to know Carole would understand.

She nestled nearer to him. "Strange as it sounds, I'm disappointed too."

"Do you want to talk about it?" He had learned they couldn't avoid their issues, and hope they would go away. They must face them, head-on. Carole was disappointed that her mother-in-law hadn't put in an appearance. Jack was surprised, but oddly pleased.

"I do. We need to make peace with her, but there's something else we have to talk about first."

Jack knew what that something else was. "Kevin Hartman, Suzanne's new boyfriend?"

"Boyfriend my Aunt Nellie." Carole sat up and turned to face him. That *boyfriend* is thirty if he's a day."

"He asked to have a private talk with me while Ralph and Otis watched the football game. We went into the den and had a long conversation. I missed seeing the Bills tramp all over the Cardinals." As an afterthought, he added, "Kevin is twenty-nine-years-old." Dread crawled up his backbone. The next bit of news he had to tell his wife would test their new-found closeness.

"I've never seen him in the store, and I've been there dozens of times. This is not good." Carole tagged her statement with a question. "Why would he want to talk to you?"

"He's not the manager of the store, he's the owner." There was no easy way to break disturbing news. "He asked for Suzanne's hand in marriage."

"We don't know this man." Carole jumped to her feet. "He may be a wanted criminal, or a wife beater, he could be a bigamist. Oh, Jack, what are we going to do?"
"He could be a serial killer, he—"
"Don't joke about this." Carole sat back down. "What did you tell him?"
Jack took her hand. "Suzanne talked to me about her and Kevin last week. She asked me not to mention it to you until after Kevin had a chance to meet you and talk to me." He gritted his teeth and waited for Carole to explode.
Instead, she asked in a calm voice, "Why didn't she want me to know?"
"She wanted you to meet Kevin first, and she didn't want to spoil your Thanksgiving."
"Was she that sure I would disapprove?" Carole moved nearer her husband.
Jack put his arm around her. She was taking this better that he thought she would. "Suzanne is going to marry Kevin. We can't stop her. She's of age. It took a lot of guts for Kevin to come here and speak to me as he did. I believe he loves our daughter. Would you like me to tell you what he said?"
"Yes. Very much."
"He's from a good family. He's the only child of Emma and Roscoe Hartman. He has been divorced. He and his high school sweetheart eloped when they were seniors. They were divorced the summer before Kevin went away to college." Jack hugged Carole closer. "We have to let go. As hard as it is. We have to let Suzanne find her own way. Cheer up, you still have me."
"You are so right," Carole admitted. "We have to let our daughter find her own way, and unfortunately, make her own mistakes. Thank you for being here and for making me see that."
Jack's heart swelled with happiness. "Thank you for staying with me through the worst period of my life, and for helping me find my way to Jesus."

ASKING FOR A MIRACLE

Carole stood, took Jack's hand and pulled him to a standing position. "I know what my wedding gift to them will be. I am giving them the house Aunt Effie left me."

"That's very generous of you."

"Does that mean you approve?"

"I can think of nothing I'd like better."

They walked hand-in-hand toward the living room door. Carole measured her pace to Jack's uneven gait.

The loud jangle of the telephone disturbed the quiet of the room.

"Who can that be at this hour?" Carole stopped and stood still.

An unwelcome jolt of anxiety skipped down Jack's spine. "Shall I answer?"

"Maybe you'd better."

Jack moved toward the telephone and picked up the receiver. "Hello."

A gruff voice sounded in his ear. "Is that you, Jack?" Before he could respond the voice softened. "This is Police Chief Nyles. I'm calling about your mother."

"What about her? Has there been an accident?" He felt Carole's hand on his shoulder. She put her ear near his.

"No accident," the police chief replied, "but you'd better get over here as soon as possible."

"Over where?"

"Over to your Mama's house. She's out in the front yard in her underwear, and she won't let anyone near her."

"I'm on my way." Jack hung up the phone and turned toward his wife. "Did you hear?"

"I heard. I'm going with you."

Chapter Thirty-Three

December 3, 1975, Wednesday Noon

Jack and Carole sat with Steve and Margie in the plush outer office of Doctor Ezra Cunningham, anxiously awaiting the final report from Clarissa's several tests and examinations. Carole looked around the room at the many awards and commendations hanging on the walls. We are waiting for a neurologist. How did it come to this? The past six days were trying ones for everyone, but her main concern was for Jack. He was recovering from a demoralizing accident and only now learning to maneuver around and walk well on his prosthesis.

She squeezed her husband's hand. "We will, with God's help get through this. A year ago, I couldn't say that. We have both suffered loss and pain. But in the process we found God, and we found each other."

Jack returned her squeeze. "All the same, I hate putting you through this."

"This is where I want to be. I won't desert you this time."

Carole's mind harked back to Thanksgiving night when, after much harangue, Jack talked Clarissa out of her front yard and into her house. Carole and Jack stayed the night with her. Neither of them slept a wink. Neither did Clarissa.

Doctor Cunningham came into his office, and nodded a greeting to the two couples before positioning himself behind his desk. "I am sorry for the wait. I had an emergency."

Margie waved his apology aside. "What is wrong with my mother? Why would she go outside in her underwear? Has she lost her mind?"

Steve patted her shoulder. "Patience my dear, patience."

"Forgive me." Margie bit her lip and looked at the floor.

"I can understand your anxiety." Doctor Cunningham laced his fingers together and put his hands on his desk. "The news in not good. Your mother's cognitive processes have been impaired. She has a brain tumor."

"What can you do? Can you operate?" Marge's voice honed the edge of hysteria.

Her outburst clashed with Jack's "There must be some mistake..." His voice faded on an intake of breath. "Why didn't I know? Why didn't I guess?"

Steve took charge. "Why don't we settle down and let Doctor Cunningham tell us the results of his tests?"

An ominous quiet settled over the group. Doctor Cunningham spoke. "We have diagnosed your mother's problem as a glioblastoma tumor."

His diagnosis hit Carole as if she had been struck by a Mack truck traveling at maximum speed. She found it difficult to breathe.

"Can you operate and remove it?" Margie leaned forward with a worried expression contorting her face.

Steve put his arm arms around his wife's shoulders and drew her close. "Let him finish."

"Yes, please do." Doctor Cunningham replied. He sighed before continuing. "This type of tumor is malignant and extremely aggressive. It forms tentacle-like appendages that make it very difficult to remove. The chance that it will reappear after surgery is almost one hundred percent. The location of your mother's tumor makes it impossible to remove without causing additional damage to her brain."

Steve, steady as always, asked what Jack, Margie, or Carole couldn't find the strength to voice, "How long Doctor?"

"A year at the most." The words fell like a sledgehammer pounding out into the quiet of the room.

Carole was the first to regain her equilibrium. "Jack and I will take care of her. We have a room in our home suitable for an ailing patient."

"I can't ask you to do this." Jack grabbed both of Carole's hands.

ASKING FOR A MIRACLE

"You are not asking." She pulled her hands free. "I am volunteering. I need to treat Clarissa with compassion. God is giving me an opportunity to make amends for past wrongs."
Jack said, "There were extenuating circumstances—"
Carole raised one hand. "Please, Jack, I want to do this."

*****

Three days later, despite Jack's misgivings and Margie's dire predictions, Clarissa had settled in the den that had been Jack's room through his long recovery.
Carole was frightened, but willing to begin her new responsibility. She had never in her life done anything that was completely unselfish. *Dear Jesus, thank you for giving me this challenging opportunity. Help me to succeed.*
In a few days Jack stopped protesting and Margie ceased to nag.
The first week of adjustment was trying. Much to Carole's surprise, Margie came on the first weekend to relieve her. "I will suffer Mother's complaints and demands for two days. You need a rest."
"Are you sure?"
"Can we talk?" Margie moved to the edge of the couch.
"About what?" Carole couldn't dismiss a nudge of suspicion.
"Steve and I are back together, really back together, and it's all because of you."
"Me?" Something was wrong here. Carole stood and paced across the floor before she turned to stare at her sister-in-law. "What did I do?"
"Would it surprise you to know I have always admired you? I have always been jealous of you, too. You were so sure of yourself. You always had everything so together. When I found Jesus as my savior, I knew with His help, I could change and be a woman like you instead of a silly teenager in a woman's body. I want us to be friends." She extended her arms "Will you hug me?"

Carole's heart melted. All these years Margie had been watching her, and what a poor example she had been. She stood and walked toward Margie. "I count it an honor to be your friend."

Chapter Thirty-Four

December 24, 1975, Wednesday Evening

Jack opened the door and stood aside to let Carole enter. "The ceremony was beautiful."

Carole removed her gloves and hat. "Otis and Midge are both so happy."

The nurse who they'd hired to stay with Clarisse during the wedding and reception, came through the living room and into the foyer. "Mrs. Garner is asleep. I gave her pain medication just before she dropped off. It should see her through the night."

"How much do I owe you?" Jack took his wallet from his hip pocket.

"Nothing. Put your money away." The nurse put her arms into her coat. "Pay it forward." Before he could object, she was out the door, and gone.

He turned to Carole. "What a gracious gesture. Who is that woman?"

"Her name is Alice Whitman. She's a friend of Ralph and Grace."

"What did she mean by 'pay it forward?'"

"It's her way of saying now it's your turn to pass a good deed on to someone else." Carole hung her coat on a hook, and yawned. "Would you like a snack or a cup of coffee?"

"I would like a piece of that coconut cake you made this morning. And maybe a glass of milk." Jack followed his wife into the kitchen. What a difference a few months had made in their relationship.

They sat at the table, eating cake, drinking milk, and reminiscing over the events of the evening. Finally, Jack asked a question he had wanted to raise since they came through the front door. "Did you talk to Suzanne and Kevin?" Carole's doubt about Suzanne's coming marriage to Kevin was the one dark spot in Jack's otherwise placid existence.

"We spoke briefly. I told them we were giving them Aunt Effie's house as a wedding present."
"We?" he questioned.
"Yes. We." Carole grimaced before adding, "At Midge's insistence, she and I had a long talk a week or so back." She picked up cake crumbs from the table with her fingers, and dropped them into her plate.
"I don't think we're on the same page." Jack ran his fingers through his hair.
"We are," Carole assured him. "Hear what I have to say."
Jack leaned back in his chair. "I'm listening. Fire away."
"Midge told me if her mother had stayed out of it, her first marriage may have succeeded. She said instead of listening to her mother pointing out all Rhett's faults, she should have concentrated on Rhett and her husband's good points. She said she told Suzanne as much, then advised her to concentrate on Kevin and their life together."
Jack chuckled. "How like Midge to speak her mind in any and all circumstances.
"That's what I thought when Midge told me what she had done. I took her to task for butting in where she had no business. She replied. 'It must be difficult to be a mother,' and walked away."
Jack thought of the indomitable woman who had been his mother, and how she was now a frail shadow of herself, lying, waiting for a cancer to eat her life away. "Mother scoffed at what she always referred to as 'organized religion. I must talk to her about her spiritual condition."
"Maybe we *aren't* on the same page." Carole shook her head. "I don't know that Midge was referring to anything spiritual."
"I'm not talking about Midge. I'm talking about Mother. Go on with what you were saying."
"I gave what Midge said a lot of thought. She was right. It is difficult to be a mother. Mothers never mean to hurt their children, but sometimes we do. I thanked her later for alerting me to some things I might

otherwise have neglected to see. I have ceased to speak ill of Kevin to Suzanne. Her marriage is her business, hers and Kevin's."

"We had the same problem when we were first married." Jack's memory skipped back over past years to remember how his mother and Carole's Aunt Effie were constantly interfering in their lives and their marriage. "It took us a while to learn to ignore them. I should amend that statement. We didn't ignore them."

"We didn't, did we?" Carole's eyes lit with love. "That was a part of our problem. Oh, Jack, think of all the years we wasted."

"One thing my journey with Jesus is teaching me is the importance of letting go of the past. Thank God we have now, and the promise of tomorrow. I love you, Carole, with every beat of my heart."

"I love you, too, more every day." Carole stood and pushed her chair under the table. "I'm going to look in on Clarissa before I go to bed. I want to be sure her intercom is on."

"I'll be waiting for you upstairs." Jack stood slowly and with some difficulty as he began his uneven gait toward the stairs. He knew he was a blessed man—so fortunate that God gave him Carole for his life's partner.

Chapter Thirty-Five

December 31, 1975, Wednesday Evening

"I'm glad we opted to stay at home tonight." Carole looked across the room toward her husband. "Midge and Otis, and Ralph and Grace are coming by after the midnight church services. They can tell us all about the Church's New Year's Program."

"It will be a welcome change to hear some good news." Jack laid his paper aside. "Sometimes I wonder why I bother to read that thing." He pointed to the paper he had so recently tossed aside. "It's full of nothing but bad news. I have been reading about the terrorist bombing at La Guardia Airport. Eleven people died in that blast."

"Not everything in the newspaper is bad news. Monday, I read a glowing account of Roger Staubach's Hail Mary pass to Drew Pearson last Sunday." Carole's aim was to make her husband smile.

He did. "That was some play—"

Clarissa's intercom buzzer sounded. Carole pushed the receive button. "Yes?"

"Get in here," Clarissa demanded. "Bring my son with you."

"Coming." Clarissa sounded like her old self, complaining and demanding. Over the past few weeks, she had alternated between recalling her past and remembering very little of what had happened before her meltdown. She'd also become somewhat more pleasant and cooperative.

Carole headed for her patient's room, reminding herself as she went to be tolerant and gentle.

Jack followed close behind.

They entered the room to find Clarissa grimacing in pain. "I need medicine."

Clarissa drew a rasping breath. "There are some things I need to say. Things I should have made know to you long ago." She waved one frail hand in a dismissive gesture. "That's in the past now. As ugly as my past is, it can't be changed."

"Mother," Jack interrupted, "How can you have a past? All you have ever been is a wife, a mother, and a civic-minded citizen."

"Ha," Clarissa snorted. "I was a rotten wife, a terrible mother, and civic-minded only when it suited my purpose."

"We can talk about this tomorrow." Carole had to put a stop to this, now. It was breaking Jack's heart, and for what? She forced a stiff smile. "We can talk about our plans for the new year."

"Carole's right," Jack chimed in. "Tomorrow is soon enough."

"Can't you two get it through your stupid heads?" Clarissa asked, "There is no tomorrow. There never was. It's always today. Shut up, the both of you, and hear what I have to say."

Clarissa's frail voice fell out into the quiet of the hovering silence. She told of her childhood, a subject she had never before mentioned. She spoke of how her father had abused her from an early age. "He was a monster. I prayed each night for God to kill him." There was no emotion in her voice. She continued her horror story in a flat, even voice.

She spoke of how her mother knew and never lifted a finger to stop him. "Mother's concerns were her looks and spending Father's money." She completed her woeful tale by saying, "I never told anyone this before."

Carole was appalled. Clarissa had been carrying this hurt and anger around inside for all these years. Small wonder she grew up to be the person she was. *Lord, forgive me.*

Clarissa closed her eyes, and opened them again. "I don't want to die without finding a way to ask God to forgive me." She pulled her hand free from Jack's grasp and touched his cheek with the tips of her cold fingers. "Tell me more, my son, about your savior, Jesus."

Her words struck Carole like a fist to her mid-section. How smug she was, as day-by-day she cared for her mother-in-law with gentle compassion. She had never once spoken to the ailing woman about Jesus. Why didn't she? The answer rang through her senses like the knell of doom. She thought Clarissa was beyond redemption. She prayed silently for Jesus to forgive her.

Jack spoke in soothing tones as he told the old sweet story of Jesus and his love. He ended by explaining the plan of salvation. "Jesus says 'Whosoever will may come to Me and I will forgive his sins and make him a child of God.' All you must do..."

Clarissa interrupted, "Does that whosoever include me?"

Carole's throat filled with tears of self-condemnation. How far short reality fell from this woman's proud self-image.

Jack took his mother's hand in his. "It means anyone who will believe that Jesus is the Son of God, and confess that belief."

"I do believe, and I confess that belief." Clarissa declared in whispered tones.

"Carole, please, pray with us." Jack held his mother's hand as emotion overcame him.

Carole bowed her head. Never had she felt so humble and unworthy. "Father God we come to thee—"

Chapter Thirty-Six

January 1, 1976, Thursday Morning

Carole sitting up in bed awakened Jack. He turned over. "Are you all right?"

Carole stood and slipped her feet into her slippers. "I thought I heard Clarissa's intercom buzz, but she doesn't answer. I'm going down to see about her."

"I'll be down soon." Jack had heard nothing. He sat on the side of the bed and reached for his prosthesis.

Fifteen minutes later he entered Clarissa's room. His mother lay still and quiet in her bed. He knew, even before he moved nearer that his mother had slipped the bonds of mortality. Her soul had taken flight to a better place.

Carole's pale face told of her angst. "She's gone."

Jack fell into the chair near the door. "She knew." He should feel sorrow. All he experienced was guilt. "I was a terrible son. I should have known. I should have been more loving, more supportive." Tears rolled unheeded, down his cheeks. "I loved her. Despite everything that happened between us, I loved her, and I failed her miserably."

"We can't change what was." Carole rushed to his side, stood beside him, and took his hands in hers. "Good things can come from bad happenings. If I had not lost Aunt Effie, I would never have set out to find my father. When I learned the man he had been, I was heartbroken. God used that experience to bring me back to Him. If you had not lost your leg you might never have come to Jesus. Sometimes God pushes us to the extreme to bring us to Him. Through your testimony Margie found Jesus and Steve returned to Him after years of straying."

Jack pulled one hand free and wiped at his tears. "We can't change what was, and we can't bring back what we had."

"We can let go of the past," Carole said. "The apostle Paul wrote in Philippians chapter three, verses thirteen and fourteen: *Brethren, I count not myself to have apprehended: but this one thing I do, forgetting those things which are behind, and reaching forth unto those things which are before, I press toward the mark for the prize of the high calling of God in Christ Jesus.*"

Light shone in Jack's heart, and peace settled over his soul. "We must use what we have now to serve and glorify our Savior."

"Yes," Carole nodded her agreement, "and we have so much. Our past experiences strengthen and support us. Our faith and trials assure us." She stood and smiled down at her husband. "We must remember in all things to give thanks. The Bible tells us this is God's will concerning us."

"Now I have many things to do." Jack went across the room and used his thumbs to close Clarissa's unseeing eyes before he covered her face with a sheet. "Thank you, Jesus for giving me the assurance that my mother now rests in peace."

Carole came to stand beside him. "I will make arrangements for the mortuary to come for Clarissa's body."

"I will go to Margie and Steve's and tell them Mother is gone." He didn't look forward to the mission ahead of him. But he was, as always, the big brother, and Margie needed him now. He came back across the room and put his arm around his beloved wife. "With God's help, we will get through this."

"Amen" She smiled up at him. "You and me and Jesus."

The End

About the Author

Billie Houston writes sweet romance and Christian themed romance novels. She is a widow, the mother of three, and the grandmother of seven wonderful grandchildren. She is also a former English teacher and has worked with special needs children.

Her venture into Christian romance began when her husband of many years fell victim to Alzheimer's. She writes romantic tales about relationships, stories that explore the problems and pleasures of living a Christian life. The plots revolve around ordinary people caught in extraordinary circumstances and faced with difficult decisions.

Billie likes poetry, George Strait's music, old movies and Earl Grey tea. Her hobbies are reading, quilting, sewing, knitting, crocheting, taking long walks, and growing house plants and herbs.

Other Books by Billie Houston

Discovering Emily
Honey in the Rock
John Jacob Worthington Jones
Lucky in Love
Old Maid Bride
Sparrow on a Housetop
Summertime in my Heart
That Scott Woman
The Potter's Wheel
The Road to Jericho

Books of Poetry:
Brush Country:
Four Part Harmony:
Chapter and Verse (Poetry)

CPSIA information can be obtained
at www.ICGtesting.com
Printed in the USA
BVHW092019270322
632588BV00007B/222

9 781955 892162